The Devil On Eighty-Five

Clark Lohr

BarZF Press

Tucson, AZ

DEDICATION

To the men and women of LEAP—Law Enforcement Against Prohibition.

To anybody who ever smoked a joint.

To the memory of "Buzz" Shook, of Ajo, Arizona, who tried to get people clean and sober.

ACKNOWLEDGEMENTS

Raymond Chandler, author of *The Big Sleep* and other novels.
Jeffrey G. Buchella, Attorney at Law.
Stan Lehman, J.D., retired.
Robert S. Blackett: Forensic Science-DNA.
The Pima County Sheriff's Department, Ajo Station.
Jim Malusa and Pete Sundt
Sherry Kiyler
Diana R. Lohr, MSW, LCSW.
Steve Cohen, MSW.
Richard Fridena, Phd.
The Federal Bureau of Investigation (FBI), Tucson office.
"Buzz" Shook
George Dodds
Jayne Kyl
David Siddall, MSW, LCSW.
Carl Formby
Barry Reflow
Lisa Chernin Newman
Scott Seckel
Charles F. Hadd, Jr.
Bakbergen Turibekov
Teresa Burrell
Law Enforcement Against Prohibition (LEAP).
The National Organization for the Reform of
Marijuana Laws (NORML).
National Drug Intelligence Center (archives)
The Drug Policy Alliance
The Tohono O'odham-English Dictionary
Matthew Cooke, Director/Writer:
How to Make Money Selling Drugs
The Arizona Daily Star
The Copper News
The New York Times: DealBook
The Guardian—UK
El Pa ís—Spain
The Narco News Bulletin
www.blogdelnarco.com

The Phoenix New Times
Doug Fine: *Too High to Fail*.
Charles Bowden, journalist, and author of many books
on the US-Mexico border and the drug trade.
Molly Molloy, researcher on Mexico's narco wars.
The Global Commission on Drug Policy
George W. Grayson, scholar and author of
books on Mexican drug cartels.
Ioan Grillo, author of
El Narco: Inside Mexico's Criminal Insurgency.
Les Jennings

"The society is so totally corrupt and the corruption is so endemic. Hammett understands immediately how interconnected the government is with the police, the police with the press, the police and the press and the government with the Mob."
--Joan Mellen, Hammett biographer, from the American Masters production *Dashiell Hammett, Detective. Writer.* Quoted with the kind permission of Joan Mellen.

Prologue

The man could not read but he could count money and the cartridges for his guns. He stood now, at a battered dresser in a small room, and placed each polished piece of ammunition on a cloth, laying out, in total, fifteen rounds.

A statuette sat above the cartridges, a carved wooden figure of a handsome, dark-haired man sitting in a chair, one hand resting on a stack of green money. The man kneeled in front of the statuette and crossed himself, finishing this act in the Spanish fashion, kissing the cross made by laying his thumb over his trigger finger.

"Jesùs Malverde," he whispered, "bless these bullets."

When he finished his prayers he fixed his blue eyes on the cartridges and loaded them into the magazine of a handgun.

A curious tourist, seeing this man on the streets of Mexico, might have wondered where the man got his eye color. Maybe from the conquistadores of northern Spain, the tourist might think, the killers who sailed with Cortez, long ago, to the New World.

The blue-eyed man never wondered where he got his eye color. He knew his father had been some client of his mother's. An American, probably. He'd never asked her about it. He'd beaten her to death in Juarez before he'd come west, to do the job.

Chapter One

"Remember Donald Donahue, that country boy Judge Struck sent up for the full nickel?" Jeffrey Goldman said to his investigator, Manuel "Manny" Aguilar, who stood like a large shadow in the middle of Goldman's law office, a bungalow in Tucson's West University neighborhood. Goldman spent his days there, fighting for the underdog, and denying that he cared about anybody but himself.

Manny heard Jeff but he wasn't listening. He was sneaking looks at Reina, a tall, green-eyed redhead who sat at her work station, her long fingers ripping out a legal abstract.

Now here's a girl who knows how to keyboard, Manny thought. Reina's breasts would shiver ever so slightly, ever so often, when she hit a key just right. Manny would wait for it, like a demented house cat waiting for a drop of water to fall off a faucet. Her keyboarding paled in comparison to the way she could bend over and open a file cabinet. He went crazy when she drank out of the water fountain. Never mind that they were both over forty and had been lovers for years. Some days, Manny just went nuts.

Reina looked up, not directly at Manny, but at the room. Her green fox's eyes bore a disgusted expression that said *stop staring and listen to the boss or forget third base for all eternity.*

"Manny," Goldman said, "do I have your attention?"

Manny came back into focus. Reina smirked and disappeared behind her flat screen.

"Donny, the Tohono O'odham cowboy," Manny said. "He'd never lived off the reservation. Moved to Tucson, took a shot at the South Tucson Aztecas. Hit one in the scrotum. Used a .22 rifle. Then the South Tucson Aztecas stopped trying to steal his car."

"Bingo," Goldman said. "Donny just finished his five years in jail for that, in spite of all I could do. Now he's back in jail. Why? Somebody killed Lois. You remember her. Nice young woman. Donny's wife. The ME has the body. Positive identification is pending but no one doubts it."

Reina stopped keyboarding and leaned out around the flat screen. "What about Jonas?"

"I'll get to that," Goldman said, and kept talking to Manny. "Donny's in jail in Sells. You can see the police logic here. Pin it on a husband with a history of violence. I'm defending Donny. He would never kill his wife and the federal courts pay me either way."

"The murder happened on the Tohono O'odham Nation?"

"Yes," Goldman said. "The TO police are holding him on an assault charge for now. Federal law does not allow the Tohono O'odham Nation to prefer murder charges. Murder charges fall under the authority of the US Attorney's office. I'm sure the TO police brought in the FBI as soon they realized they were looking at a murder and there is every indication that a murder charge is imminent in Donald Donahue's case."

Manny gave Goldman a tired nod and waited for the lawyer to keep talking.

"As for cooperation from the FBI, there is none. We'll be relying on the leavings from the federal prosecutor." Goldman paused and tried to suppress a smile. He failed. "The TO police may cooperate with you in a guarded fashion. Since you work for the defense, both agencies already hate you—but you know that. Good luck with it. You're cleared to go to Sells and interview Donald Donahue. Stop looking at Reina and get to work." Goldman spun around so fast his ponytail flipped. He went into his office and closed the door.

Manny felt a thing like a wind inside him and he was hearing his Yaqui grandmother's laughter in his head. *Wake up, boy, you slept in your mind.* She was laughing at him. Her grandson, the simpleton who alerted like a dog whenever a big hunt was on. A big American dog with a broken nose that had healed just a little crooked. A scary-smart dog, as law dogs went. But still a dog, with a lot of barking up the wrong saguaros ahead of him. He nodded to Reina and headed for the door.

"Come here," Reina whispered, crooking a finger. They kissed. They kissed again. "Ask Donny about Jonas," Reina said. "See you tonight." She grabbed his butt and then let go. He walked into the winter sunlight of Tucson, Arizona, feeling like somebody had stuck a light bulb in his jeans.

***

Manny got in his Ford truck and drove the sixty-odd miles to Sells, where he endured the process of presenting identification and being generally inspected.

Eventually, Manny sat down in an interview room with Donald "Donny" Donahue, a husky man of medium height who moved with that certain considered grace characteristic of cowboys.

"Donny, how long you been here?"

"Two days." Donny's voice was hard, ragged.

"Where were you arrested?"

"At ranch headquarters. They didn't tell me why they were after me until they got me in the cage car. The FBI wasn't going to let me unsaddle my horse. The TO police told the FBI to shove it. I unsaddled my horse and brushed him down. You should of seen the FBI. They were pissed. I told all them sons of bitches I wanted a lawyer."

Manny kept asking questions. Donald Donahue had ridden out of tribal herd headquarters alone on the afternoon the murder. He'd returned after dark, the early dark of a winter evening on the Sonoran desert. He'd seen no one, he said, and no one had seen him. He'd neither made nor received cell phone calls.

During interviews conducted by his arresting officers he'd come to understand that his wife's murder occurred when he was out riding. He had not been far from the dirt road where somebody killed Lois Donahue—that is to say the TO Police believed it was Lois Donahue's charred remains which they had found in her black Toyota Tercel.

The next morning, sitting in jail in Sells, Donny realized that the weather had turned to fog and hard rain. Now the hoofmarks of his horse were washed away. Not even the Shadow Wolves, the elite Native trackers who hunted drug and human smugglers on the Tohono O'odham Nation, could testify to Donny's whereabouts on the previous day.

Manny went through the last few questions. "Donny can you think of anybody who'd want to hurt Lois?"

"Nope." Donahue looked away and his eyes filled with tears.

"Did she say anything about doing anything new?" Manny asked. "Did she have any new associates? Did her routines change? Was there anything you noticed her doing that was out of the ordinary?"

"Lois just took care of business. Took Jonas to first grade and picked him up every day. Did some part time work in town."

"Where?"

"That coffee house. The Ban 'eldag Café. They got a little art gallery there."

"How's Jonas? Reina says she wants to know."

Donahue ducked his head and cleared his throat. "He's okay....he's okay. He's with Evelyn, uh, Evelyn Antone. She's Lois's...Lois's sister. Tell Reina 'thanks.'" Donahue looked into a corner.

"I'd like to contact Evelyn," Manny said. "I'd also like to talk to Jonas, if that's okay with you. Maybe get somebody in who knows how to interview little kids. Can I do that?"

"Yeah, I guess so," Donny said. "You want Evelyn's number?"

Manuel Aguilar took down Evelyn Antone's phone number. "Donny, could you call Evelyn and give her a heads up? Let her know I'll be contacting her?"

"Yeah. You think Jonas knows something I don't?"

"He might. He was with her while you were away."

"*Away*? I was in prison for busting an arrow in a Mexican car thief's ass."

4

"Donny, would you take a lie detector test about all this stuff?"

"Yeah," Donny said. "I told the TO police I would. I told them to give me one right there and get me my lawyer. The FBI asked me the same question. I told them, too."

"Guess they shouldn't have told you that you couldn't unsaddle your horse," Manny said.

"Damn right," Donald Donahue said.

***

Reina looked up from her latest personal project to see Jeff Goldman coming toward her desk. He'd been restless for most of the day. She knew why and she quietly resolved to torture him about it later.

Neither of them had much to do. Mostly, they were waiting for Manny to get back from Sells with the word on Donny Donahue.

"What are those?" Goldman said, seeing several sets of neatly stacked cards on Reina's desk. "Are those flash cards? Did you miss that part about learning the times tables in grade school?"

Reina brightened. "Oh! These are my Mexican cartel bosses flash cards. Want to test me on them?"

Jeff reached for a stack of cards.

"No, not those," Reina said. "Those are my murdered Mexican journalist flash cards."

"I'd rather test you on the murdered Mexican journalists," Goldman said. "I have to hear federal prosecutors name Mexican cartel bosses at least once a week in federal court—where ninety-percent of the drug smuggling cases are for nothing more than marijuana. The prosecutors think it makes my clients look like the United States isn't the market for all that cannabis."

Reina dug a third stack of cards out a drawer. "Let's compromise. How about we drill with these Mexican cartel *plaza bosses* flashcards? Shorty Guzman's boys who're right on the

Arizona border? Let's see, as of May, 2013, we see Guillermo Nieblas Nava running the Sonoyta Plaza, just across the border from Organ Pipe Cactus National Monument, 40 short miles from Ajo. And our neighbor in Nogales, Sonora, 70 miles from Tucson, Felipe de Jesus Sosa Canisales, boss of, you guessed it, the Nogales Plaza, and—"

"American drug warrior flash cards?" Goldman asked. "Private prison flash cards?"

"All in good time," Reina said. "Let's just go with murdered Mexican journalists."

Goldman picked up the stack of murdered Mexican journalists cards. "Daniel Alejandro Martínez Balzadúa."

"Worked for *Vanguardia*. April 2013. Body mutilated. Motive unconfirmed."

"Jaime Guadalupe González Domínguez."

"*OjinagaNoticias*, March 2013. Shot dead in street. Motive unconfirmed."

"Where does this notation 'motive unconfirmed' come from?" Goldman asked.

"The Committee to Protect Journalists," Reina said.

"Judging from the size of this stack of flash cards," Goldman said, "the committee isn't doing so well. How about Regina Martínez Pérez?"

"Wrote articles on the drug cartels for *Proceso*, a hoity-toity Mexican magazine. April 2012. Body in bathtub. Beaten, strangled. 'Motive unconfirmed.' She was 49 years old—and as of April 2012, she was the 40th reporter killed since Calderón took office in 2006."

"Do we have any confirmed motives in this stack of cards, Reina, or is it just a great big murder mystery we can all play at— except for those of us who are Mexican journalists, their friends and families, and maybe a bunch of killjoys—not to make a pun of it—like Homicide Survivors, Inc., who think, like me, that murder mysteries aren't particularly entertaining?"

"Sure, lots of confirmed motives," Reina said. "Keep flipping."

"Oh, here's one now. I'll read you the flip side and you tell me the name."

"I can't," Reina said. "There are so many journalists killed in Mexico that I can't go by month and year and the newspaper they worked for."

"Okay. 'Adrián Silva Moreno. Freelance journalist. November 14, 2012.'"

"He goes down as 'motive confirmed' because there is evidence he was murdered in direct reprisal for his work."

"What was he doing?"

"Investigating cartel gasoline thefts from the army."

"Who killed him?"

"Could have been the cartel or the army. They're kind of the same thing in Mexico these days. He saw the army guys and the cartel guys. He was shot dead right there."

Goldman glanced at his watch. "I'm getting tired of playing murdered journalists. It's four-thirty. I'm out of here at five. Where's Manny?'

"I've got flashcards for banks who launder drug money," Reina said. "The Hong Kong and Shanghai Banking Corporation agreed to pay $1.92 billion to settle accusations that it laundered drug money taken in at its Mexico branches. The state and the feds debated long and hard on whether or not to file criminal charges."

"Then they didn't. I remember. They settled in 2012. If they put HSBC in criminal court they'd ruin a bank big enough to destabilize the global financial system. Nobody loves the drug wars more than me. You couldn't make this stuff up." He glanced at his watch. "Where's our investigator?"

***

Jeff Goldman was leaving the office when Manny got back from Sells at 5 o'clock.

"How did it go?" Goldman asked, fumbling with his top coat.

"I got a verbal okay from Donny to talk to his son," Manny said.

"We can't do that directly. Legal issue. Interview Lois's sister, Evelyn Antone. You can do that. I'll set it up. Did Donny tell you he'd take a lie detector test?" Goldman was busily patting down the collar of his top coat.

"He said he'd take one," Manny said.

"Good. He's innocent. We know that. Why did they arrest him so fast—aside from assuming that he'd kill his wife because he once fired a .22 rifle at a bunch of little gangbangers who were stealing his car?"

"He argued with them," Manny replied. "Told them he wanted his lawyer. You know what happens when law enforcement hears that you want a lawyer. They arrest you if they can. He's an ex-convict now. He's edgy. He's defensive."

"He just lost his wife," Reina added, from behind her flat screen.

"Another country heard from," Goldman said, tossing the comment in Reina's direction. Goldman was fiddling with the belt on the top coat now. Manny began to wonder why his boss was so agitated. "Where was he when the murder happened?" Goldman said. "Did he see anybody when he was out riding? Did he use his cell phone so we can ask for a GPS reading?" Goldman glanced at Reina, who was now leaning around her monitor and smiling at him in an odd way.

"I could map the area where Donny was riding." Manny offered. "I could ask around out there. Donny says he didn't use his cell. He says he couldn't get reception so he didn't try."

"If you can, get into that area of the Tohono O'odham Nation when you, as a matter of formality, make your next trip to Sells, where you will talk to the TO police and probably learn nothing. Not to micromanage, but make sure you put 'went there, learned nothing' in your report. We should have a Medical Examiner's report very soon. I believe you know Brady Pogue at the ME's office. Call him, if you will. Find out what was done to Lois Donahue. I'm out of here. See you tomorrow." Goldman glanced at Reina again. She still had that odd smile. "*What*, Reina?"

"Women are information gathering entities, Jeff," Reina said sweetly. "You've said so yourself."

"So you know. One of the desk jockeys at the prosecuting attorney's office told you."

"No, one of the waiters at the Cup Café in the Hotel Congress. How could you do it, Jeff?"

"What, have dinner with an attorney on the prosecutor's staff?"

"The waitress told me you had dinner. The desk clerk told the waitress you got a room."

"I'd advise discretion, Reina," Jeff said. "And a little comportment. Why do you bring this up now?"

"You were just so nervous. I understand she's a very nice woman, Jeff. And very attractive. But how do you get by her sharp teeth?"

"The same way she gets by mine," Jeff said. "Instead of gossiping, you might conference with our investigator on saving Donald Donahue from a life sentence. And please take note that the wooden and metal plaque you recently placed on your desk was designed to display your name, Reina, and not the words 'Give Polytheism a Chance.'"

"Speaking of Spirit, I've always meant to ask you, Jeff," Reina said, "given your rebellious, iconoclastic nature, how was your bar mitzvah?"

"I give you back the question," Goldman said, turning to deal with his statuesque, smart mouthed paralegal. "How was your sacrament of confirmation?"

"Touché," Reina said. "I was drunk."

"So, since you present yourself as some kind of mystic witch," Goldman waved an imaginary wand, "conjure up a bar mitzvah roughly as embarrassing for my parents as your confirmation was for yours—but without the alcohol abuse."

"Give me a break, Jeff," Reina said. "I was only *twelve*. I couldn't have done it *sober*. By the way, you're a nicer person since you've been dating her," Reina said to the attorney's now retreating back. She slid her plaque closer to the edge of her desk. "He is nicer," she said to Manny when Jeff had shut the door.

Manny put on a faux solemn face. "Why do you think that is?"

"Shut up," Reina said. "Let's go home."

***

Reina lived in a California style bungalow set back from the street and tucked behind thick white walls. Manny had gotten used to the place. It hadn't been the hardwood floors, the expensive kilims which lay on them, or the fireplace tiled in a dark blood red that put him off. He'd gradually realized that the walls changed colors, especially at night. Then there was the little water closet where he heard voices and felt wind blow across his face.

He'd talked to Reina about all of it. She'd told him that, essentially, they were having the same hallucination. She'd wanted him to be happy about that. He hadn't been. He'd done some yelling, and then realized he needed to accept whatever forces played around the lair of this woman who he loved more than he'd ever loved anybody.

The altars were okay with him, now. The incense, the odd, dark books in leather covers—all routine, for Reina. She was psychic—precognitive, at times. When strong light caught her eyes at night they glowed, causing Manuel Aguilar to wonder if he were sleeping with someone who was not entirely human. It had been a lot for an in-the-box thinker, a law enforcement person, to accept. He'd managed.

The dog and the cat were normal, even if Reina and her house were not. Goldie, the golden retriever, waited for them just inside the door, wagging her tail. Grayboy, the cat, appeared in the kitchen, yowling for food.

Later, while they were lying together in Reina's bedroom and watching tree shadows write Japanese characters on her walls, Reina asked her sometimes silent and reticent lover a question. "So what's up with the Tohono O'odham police?"

"It's a back and forth," Manny said. "When I worked for the sheriff's department we'd get pursuits down around Ajo Road that ran into the Tohono O'odham Nation. Some days they'd let us come in, other days they'd tell us they needed us to ask permission. They don't like outsiders. It's just is the way it is." He yawned.

"Well, you can kind of see why it is the way it is," Reina said. "Let's backtrack to the European conquest, the theft of their rivers and lands, the denigration of their religion. We can then move forward to the current militarization of their nation by our government as a dysfunctional response to drug and human smuggling."

"They don't have a river," Manny said.

"They *did*," Reina replied. "And the white guys dammed it up. They had the Gila, the Colorado, the Santa Cruz, and they're still suing and settling over it all."

"Please, baby," Manny muttered. "I need to get some rest."

"Honey, you're part Yaqui. A little cognizance and empathy here."

"I know there's history—"

"*Bad* history," Reina interjected. "And the feds are all over the nation these days."

"I know Homeland Security is all over the nation these days. I've just got a job to do here and now, Reina. All kinds of people live out there on the Tohono O'odham Nation. All I can do is treat them like anybody else."

Reina slid a hand along Manny's thigh. "So how do you investigate if you can't get any cooperation from TO police?"

"I'll get some cooperation from the TO police, but I'll start at the other end," Manny said. "All investigations start at zero. It's just a bigger zero when a PI starts on a rez case. No big deal. I started with Donny. He's the other end. I'll just keep asking people around the case, that's all. And we'll get something in the discovery process. You know that, you're a paralegal."

"Why are you so bitchy? Let's call Johnny Oaks about Jonas," Reina said. "And don't say 'rez case.'"

"Everybody else does, "Manny mumbled. He brushed her cheek with his slightly crooked nose, and fell asleep.

Chapter Two

Johnny Oaks appeared in Goldman's office the next morning as if summoned. He was a large man with a talent for not taking up space. He wore a cowboy hat, boots, jeans, and a Pendleton coat that, at the moment, was hung up on the handle of a holstered N-frame Smith and Wesson revolver the size of a coal shovel. The gun meant he was working.

Reina jumped up and gave Oaks a hug. Manny shook Johnny's hand.

"I see from the big black gun that you're working today," Jeff Goldman said. "When can you break loose to help us with a kid?"

"I'd like to hear the story," Oaks said. Working with Reina, Jeff and Manny meant Big Trouble. Oaks knew it.

"So you heard from the prosecutor's office, Jeff?" Reina put in.

"Yes," Goldman said. "Keep checking the fax machine. It's on its way."

Reina turned away from the men to check the fax machine, then winked at Manny and mouthed *Inside Contacts* when she was safely behind Jeff's back. Not satisfied with that, she mouthed *In Bed with the Prosecution*, followed by *Sleeping with the Enemy*. Manny was obliged to ignore her.

"I'm defending a guy from the nation," Goldman told Oaks. "He's accused of murdering his wife—"

"The murder happened on the nation?" Oaks asked, knowing that this would complicate any investigation by any outside agency or individual.

"Yes," Goldman said. "I have the prosecutor's permission to interview my client's sister-in-law. She's keeping his son. The kid is five. His name is Jonas. We can't get permission to talk to the boy. Legal issue. His mother is dead and his father is the accused murderer. You see our problem here."

"I can't do anything," Oaks said. "I'm a licensed PI. I've got the same rules you've—"

"You can ride-along," Reina said, inserting her long body into the circle of males. "Just observe. You *know* kids, Johnny. It's your specialty."

"I know teenagers," Johnny said. "I don't know a lot about little kids."

"You've been trained to interview children, Johnny. That was part of your master's degree," Reina said.

"It's been a long time," Johnny said. "You'll probably be taping the interview. The prosecutor can legally attend the meeting. They can tape it, too. I shouldn't even be there, Reina."

"Evelyn Antone, the sister-in-law, is in Sells. We'll talk there," Manny said. "She's taking care of Jonas and Jeff can clear you with the prosecutor's office."

Johnny looked even more skeptical. "Sells? What am I supposed to be doing?"

"Watching the kid," Jeff said, sticking his hands out, palms up, and waving them up and down. "Watch him play. If he's drawing something, look at what he's drawing. Observe and report. How hard is that?"

"Just watch the kid, Johnny. See what you can pick up," Manny said.

"Don't think of this as Big Trouble, Johnny," Reina said. "Think of it as an adventure for a good cause."

Chapter Three

The sign read "Police Department." No city name, only a circular symbol above, in brick red, the Man in the Maze. To the Tohono O'odham, the Desert People, this was I'itoi, the Elder Brother—a human figure standing at the starting point of a puzzle. Two flags flew from the top of the flat roof. The Stars and Stripes fluttered at the top of the pole. No surprise there. Below it, the TO nation's flag, half yellow, half purple. A red staff ran diagonally across the flag. Eleven feathers hung from a strap below the staff, one feather for each district of the reservation. Manny and Johnny Oaks were now in Sells, Arizona, the headquarters of the Tohono O'odham Nation, the third largest Indian reservation in the United States.

The passenger door on Manny's Ford creaked when Oaks got out of the truck.

"Ever think about getting a new truck?" Oaks asked as they shuffled across the parking lot toward the entrance.

"No," Manny said. "My truck's not old. It's just *older*."

A female clerk smiled while Oaks and Manny Aguilar stated their business. She told them to wait when they asked for a TO officer. Oaks and Aguilar stood and waited. There were no chairs.

Ten minutes later a uniformed lieutenant with white skin came through a secured interior door and stared at Oaks and Manny Aguilar. His eyes didn't go with his skin. His eyes were yellow and fierce and looked like they'd been lifted off the face of a Comanche. Manny was very sure, watching this guy come toward him, that mixed racial heritage was the last thing on the lieutenant's mind.

"Follow me," the lieutenant said. He took a few steps down a hallway, turned right, and disappeared through a door. Oaks opened the door and Manny followed him in, finding the lieutenant seated at the table with a file spread open in front of him.

"My name's Norris," he said. "I'm a Criminal Investigator, along with other duties as assigned. Tell me what you want to know."

"What evidence of homicide did you find at the scene?" Manny asked.

"People don't usually burn themselves up in cars," Norris said. "Our guy in the patrol unit saw fresh brass lying on the shoulder of the road—and footprints indicating someone had taken a firing stance and opened up on the vehicle. The windshield blew up in the fire so we don't know if rounds were fired through the windshield. Forensics will figure it out."

"What caliber was the brass?" Manny asked.

"Talk to the federal prosecutor's office about that. I had patrol officers secure the scene. I called for an FBI Evidence Response Team. The prosecutor's office has the details. You know that. Anything else?" Norris was staring at them the way you stare at a big green horsefly that's sucking blood out of your favorite pony.

"Did your CI's and the FBI Agents talk to anybody in the community about this?" Manny asked.

Norris shook his head in disgust. "What do you think? That's what we do. We talked to Evelyn Antone after we interviewed and arrested Donald Donahue. We notified Antone that her sister was dead. We also told her we'd charged Donald Donahue with aggravated assault and jailed him. We're talking to everybody around this case. You're cleared to interview Antone today. You've already interviewed Donald Donahue. Anything else?"

Manny was getting tired of Norris. He asked his next questions just to needle the guy. "Were you the CI who interviewed Donahue at the tribal herd stables?"

"I was one of them."

"Did either you or the FBI tape record that conversation?"

"The FBI isn't required to tape record interviews in those situations and neither am I."

"Do you have a copy of your written report for me?" Manny

asked.

"My report is your business only if the federal prosecutor's office says it is. Any more questions?"

Why are you such a dick was the obvious question but Manny and Oaks didn't ask that one. The already knew the answer: business as usual on the TO rez when it came to outsiders.

They headed out to interview Evelyn Antone.

***

Evelyn Antone lived alone in a small house outside of Sells. She was a fidgety bird of a woman who wore black horn rimmed glasses. She liked to talk. A small boy played at her feet, his toys taking up a big patch of her small living room—Jonas, the little boy whose mother wasn't coming home.

Evelyn told Oaks and Aguilar to sit and then she looked at Johnny Oaks. The big man had high cheekbones, dark eyes, and straight black hair, combed flat on top and almost reaching his collar. "Where are you from?" she asked.

Johnny ducked his head and ran his hand over his hair. "I grew up around Tahlequah, Oklahoma," he said. "I'm Cherokee."

Evelyn nodded. Manny started asking questions. Oaks watched Jonas play.

Manny got details about Evelyn's murdered sister, Lois Donahue. Manny chased the chronology. What was the dead woman's routine? Had she changed her routine? Did Lois mention having any new friends? When did Evelyn last see Lois? When did the TO police notify Evelyn of Lois's probable death, pending positive identification? Lois Donahue had a led a routine life. Lois worked part time at the Ban 'eldag Cafe and took care of Jonas. One day the school called Evelyn. Jonas hadn't been picked after class. Evelyn picked Jonas up. TO police came by that night with the bad news.

Manny got into the area of sense memories. What was Lois wearing just before she disappeared? Evelyn Antone responded with a lot of feminine details. Lois had pretty hair. Lois used certain products on her hair. She, Evelyn, had always looked up to Lois. Lois was her big sister. There were four little Antones. Two brothers and two sisters. Lois was the oldest. The two brothers were just boys who acted like boys—mean all the time. Lois protected Evelyn. Evelyn was the little sister.

"What are your brothers doing these days?" Manny asked.

"Chester lives in Sells. He works for the tribe. Joaquin's dead." Manny scrawled the names down. Chester Antone, as a relative, was statistically more likely to kill his sister than someone who didn't know her. As for Joaquin, it might be worthwhile to make sure he was really dead.

"What does Chester do?" Manny asked.

"He's a janitor out at the high school," Evelyn said.

"Do you have contact information for him?" Manny asked. "Cell phone number?"

"Yeah, guess so," Evelyn said. She picked up a cell phone lying on the arm of the couch, frowned, and punched at the thing until she found a number she read off to Manny.

"Did Lois go to Ajo much?" It was Johnny Oaks's first question of the interview.

Evelyn faltered. No more hair talk. "Sometimes," she said.

"Why?" Manny asked.

"I don't know, shopping, maybe. We all go to Ajo, sometimes."

"Do you know if she had friends in Ajo?" Manny asked.

"Lois didn't have anybody else," Evelyn snapped. "Lois wore Danny's ring every day of her life." She paused. "Let's not talk about it. I don't want to cry in front of Jonas."

Manny and Oaks were pretty well done asking Evelyn Antone questions. Evelyn Antone was pretty well done answering them, but there was one more question and Manny asked it as gently as he could.

"Evelyn," Manny said, "is there any chance Lois could have been involved in anything illegal?"

Lois shook her head, reached for a handkerchief, and pressed it to her face. "You guys come out here," she said, "and you think we're all dope smugglers or we're bringing Mexican people across the border."

"We're working for Donny," Manuel Aguilar said. "We're here to clear Donny. Anything you could tell us would help him." He waited, but Evelyn Antone was done talking.

Manny shut off his tape recorder and thanked her. The two PI's drove back to Sells. Manny cruised a slow loop through town, heading west.

"What about Ajo?" Manny asked Oaks.

Oaks opened the creaking door of Manny's Ford to free a seatbelt strap. "This seatbelt is looking for dimes," Oaks said. "Jonas was wearing an Ajo souvenir T-shirt. He had a couple other souvenirs with his toys. Ajo is seventy miles from Sells. Ajo is a one supermarket town. Tucson is closer. We've got a million people."

"Did Jonas look like a normal kid to you? Reina will want to know."

"He looks like a normal kid," Oaks said. "I watched the way he used his toys. I don't think he's been abused. I don't think he has any learning disabilities. It would take a specialist to evaluate that. All I can do is tell Reina what I saw."

"We'll talk to Evelyn Antone again," Manny said.

"We're headed away from Tucson," Oaks said. "You taking the long way to 86?"

"Ban 'eldag Café," Manny said, staring straight ahead.

"Maybe get a coffee," Oaks said, sealing an unstated accord that they would violate procedure together by trying to sneak information out of anyone they found working at the Ban 'eldag Café, the last place Lois Antone had worked.

***

The Ban 'eldag Café and Gallery sat on one end of a U-shaped shopping mall and it was a clean little piece of generic southwestern architecture. Graphics in earth tones on a stucco false front, also in earth tones. Security cameras high up on one corner. Oaks and Manny Aguilar took it all in, mentally ticking off the reasons for the cameras: art is valuable, taggers are ubiquitous, recreational violence is always a possibility.

Manny and Oaks slid their cowboy boots across the parking lot, opened the glass doors, ordered coffees, and tried to strike up a conversation with the barista about Lois Donahue, avoiding leading questions as much possible and remaining mindful of an alleged Tohono O'odham cultural custom: "Yes is better than no," a conflict avoidance strategy for a collective culture. That custom was not being employed by the barista. Other than establishing Lois Donahue's previous employment there, they got no information. A man standing fifteen feet away in the art gallery picked up a phone.

Oaks and Manny were sledding their cowboy boots back across the parking lot, coffees in hand, when the yellow-eyed lieutenant pulled up in a cruiser. "You were cleared to interview Evelyn Antone. That's all." He pointed north. "State Route 86 is that way. Get out before you screw up your own case. Do not let the screen door hit you in the ass, gentlemen."

Chapter Four

"Why would she go to Ajo?" Reina asked. Oaks and Manny sat in Jeff Goldman's office, in front of Reina's desk. Goldman himself was off at court. Oaks and Manny leaned back in their chairs, two big men in wrangler jeans and snap button shirts. Oaks had his black cowboy hat tipped back on his head. "Did she have a lover out there?" Reina went on. "Danny was in prison for five years. It happens."

"Could be, but Evelyn told us Lois was waiting for Danny," Manny said. "Evelyn said Lois wore Danny's ring every day. I believed her. I need to go to Ajo, ask some questions, show Lois's picture to people. I don't know anybody from the Pima County Sheriff's Department out there, yet. You know anybody in Ajo, Johnny?"

Oaks shook his head. "I've been out there. Hunted bighorn sheep in the Ajo Mountains a long time ago."

"I know a guy who's lived in Ajo," Reina said. "If he doesn't know the town well enough he'll put you onto somebody who does."

"What's his name and where can I find him?"

"His name is George. I'll call him for you."

"How do you know him?" Manny asked.

"Jealous?"

"No. Curious," Manny said.

Oaks leaned sideways in his chair and put a hand over his mouth to hide a smile.

"I don't know him well. I just know him from my meditation group," Reina said. "You'll like George. He's a real guy. He was backpacking in the Sierra Nevadas before anybody else was doing it. He traveled in India. He's walked the dharma for a long time."

"The what?"

"The Buddhist spiritual path."

"Do I take my boots off when I go in his house?"

"No, you buy some sandals and wear them on your head, smartass. I'll call him for you." She turned away from Manny and put her warm green eyes on Johnny Oaks. "What did Jonas look like to you, Johnny? Is he okay?"

"Looks like a normal kid to me," Johnny said.

Manny's cell phone vibrated. He glanced at the number, held up one finger, and put the phone to his ear. Reina looked at him, waiting. Oaks crossed his arms, took a breath, and stared off into middle distance.

Manny listened, thanked the caller, and snapped the phone shut. "That was Brady Pogue at the ME's office. It's Lois Donahue, confirmed. He says they got DNA from the sister—Evelyn."

"Did they get Lois's ring?" Reina asked.

"What ring?" Manny asked.

"The ring you just told me about. The wedding ring Evelyn told you Lois Donahue wore every day, Manny. You guys ever hear of the Triangle Shirtwaist Factory fire?"

Manny and Oaks stared at her.

"It happened in New York City in 1911. It killed one-hundred and forty-six people, most of them women," Reina said." Now we farm out garment work to the Third World and *those* women die in fires. People burn up, rings—"

"I'll call Pogue back," Manny said, and hit speed dial on his cell phone. "They'll take another look at the X-rays," he said, after he'd hung up. "Pogue says he'll call about the car, too. May take time. It's in DPS impound on Valencia Road."

Reina flicked her eyes at the clock on her monitor. "Qutting time. Join us for dinner, Johnny?"

"Where?" Oaks asked.

"Rosa's," Reina said.

***

At Rosa's Mexican Food Restaurant the tables were wrought of metal and the table tops themselves were done in colorful tile.

Rich, sensuous Mexican calendars hung behind the cash register. Murals graced the walls. Small numerals painted into the murals marked the table numbers. Oaks and Manny hammered down beef chimichangas and beer while Reina wondered about their arteries and picked at a Topopo Salad.

Jeff Goldman had joined them on his way to the foothills apartment of his new girlfriend. He ordered a plate of enchiladas and Manny caught Jeff up on the interview with Evelyn Antone and the indications that Lois Donahue may have been spending time in Ajo. Then Manny's phone vibrated and he snapped it to his ear.

"Pogue at the ME's office says they checked the X-rays. Lois Donahue is missing her ring finger," Manny said, when he got off the phone. "DPS checked what's left of her car. They didn't find the ring. It might still be somewhere in the wreck, but I doubt it."

"That put a whole new spin on my dinner," Reina said.

"You were picking at it, anyway," Goldman said, speaking into his plate of enchiladas.

Reina gave Goldman a withering look and addressed the assembled company of head-down male food shovelers. "I realize it's feeding time for you men here at table number eleven, but what's your collective take on that kind of mutilation?"

Manny shrugged, while chewing. "Somebody wanted the ring," he said. "Very few criminals will cut off a finger to get a ring. It means he's a real bad guy." He tore a hot corn tortilla out of a foil wrapper and used it to mop salsa off his plate.

Oaks shook his head when Reina looked at him. Goldman stayed with his enchiladas.

"So is this just robbery and murder? Or could it be drug cartels?" Reina asked.

"The cartels like to cut off heads," Manny said, his voice muffled by a mouthful of corn tortillas. "Sometimes they'll put them in a washtub full of pozole."

"So it couldn't be a guy who was real mad at his wife?" Reina asked.

"In rare cases husbands have done mutilations of that type,"

Goldman said. "We can speculate that Donald Donahue cut off his own wife's ring finger. Donny was in the area where his wife's body was found. Since we are speculating here, Reina, she could have been killed elsewhere and driven to the area where her car and her body were found, creating the appearance of opportunity on Donald Donahue's part. The FBI Evidence Response Team may be able to tell if Lois was killed elsewhere. Nevertheless, the prosecution will have to prove motive. I suspect they will have difficulty in doing so, based on what we know about Donny's relationship with his wife.

"Our investigators," Goldman went on, pointing, in turn, at Oaks and Aguilar with his fork, "will continue to look into Lois Donahue's activities and associations prior to her murder. Although she could have been killed for any number of reasons, I suspect there's more involved here than the theft of a ring."

"I'll be calling George, Manny," Reina said. "He can get you into the social whirlwind of Ajo."

Manny nodded and peeled another tortilla out of its foil wrapper. "I think we should talk with Evelyn Antone again."

"I'll set up an interview," Jeff said. "If she's withheld information she may be more forthcoming when she understands the implications the prosecution might make out of that particular kind of mutilation," Goldman said.

Reina dropped her head and gave her Topopo Salad a listless look. "Always a pleasure to see a murder investigation humming along. Can't help but think how it might feel to be the sister of a murder victim and find myself under a lot of cross examination."

"Donald Donahue could get a death sentence," Goldman said. His voice was gentle now, and kind. "It's unlikely—because he will be tried, if he is tried, under federal law—but it's possible. If he were not a Native, if he were under Arizona state law, he'd be a *perfect* candidate for a death sentence, since mutilation and burning falls under the Arizona guidelines for such a sentence. If Evelyn Antone has information, it's in Donald Donahue's best interest that we have it."

"They haven't cleared Evelyn Antone," Oaks said.

His companions looked startled.

"Manny?" Jeff asked.

"I didn't ask. That was a mistake. We got no cooperation from the TO lieutenant we talked to. He kept telling us to talk to the federal prosecutor."

"Pursuant to that," Goldman said, "you might ask for a transcript of the interview with Donald Donahue—if the TO police have it. They won't give it to you, but it won't hurt to ask. The FBI isn't required by law to tape record interviews. 'He said he did it' is sufficient in court—if you're the FBI. The defense must produce tape recordings."

Chapter Five

Manuel Aguilar's second interview with Evelyn Antone took place in an interview room at the Tohono O'odham police station with counsel for the prosecution present and armed with tape recorders. Antone herself wanted it that way.

Manny put it on the line for Evelyn. "I have some bad news for you. Your sister's ring finger was cut off and the ring is missing. It's possible that the ring will be found in the burned vehicle. I doubt that, Evelyn. I believe someone cut off Lois Donahue's finger to get her ring."

Evelyn Antone hands shook when she pushed her black horn rimmed glasses up on her nose.

"Do you see how this looks for Donny?" Manny asked. "Your brother- in- law, Donald Donahue, is the only current suspect in your sister's murder and Lois's murder is now a heinous crime under Arizona law. He'd get the death penalty—if he were tried in state court. Instead, he'll be tried in federal court—where it's extremely unlikely he'd get a death sentence—but you can rest assured he'd be a very old man before he got out of prison—his prior conviction in a shooting will guarantee that."

Manny paused, sat back in his chair, and affected the appearance of gazing into the past. "I've known Donny for over five years," he said, finally. "I've met Lois. One time we talked about their wedding day, back before Jonas was born. Your brother-in-law, Donald Donahue, slipped a wedding ring on your sister's finger. You were at that wedding, Evelyn. Do you believe your brother-in-law would cut off the wedding ring that you watched him put on your sister's finger—after he'd shot her to death? Then burn her body up in her own car?" Manny leaned forward in his chair and looked Evelyn Antone in the eyes. "Do you think Donny's that kind of man? What do you think?"

Evelyn put her face in her hands and said nothing.

Manny started bluffing. "Lois's death has every appearance of a planned, purposeful murder. When we talked the other day, you said you could think of no reason why she would be driving on the road where she was killed. I think she had a reason. I do not think this is a random murder, a crime of opportunity. I do not think Donny committed the crime. I know that Donny—the man you know as Jonas's father and your brother-in-law—will probably receive a life sentence for this crime unless someone can prove he didn't do it. I think you know something about Lois and Ajo, Evelyn. If you do know anything, this would be a good time to tell me."

Evelyn took her hands away from her face. "I don't know anything," she said.

***

Manny met George Amundsen, Reina's Ajo contact, for Mexican food at La Indita, on Fourth Avenue. The Goldman law firm was buying a midafternoon lunch in exchange for information. Amundsen was a tall white man, an easy six-four. Long hairs leapt from each eyebrow, pointing out in opposite directions like sabers.

"How long did you live in Ajo?" Manny asked, after he'd ordered a plate of heart stopping chili rellenos and George had ordered something vegetarian.

"I didn't quite in live in Ajo," George said, as if he were telling a ten-year-old a joke. "I lived in Why."

Manny waited for George to tell him What about Why.

The waitress brought iced tea and George took a sip. "Why is a village. It's southeast of Ajo, right at a "Y" where State Route 86 runs into 85. It's more of a "T" now. Some people say Why is called *Why* because it's at a "Y" in the road. Some people say it's because the tourists always asked us "Why do you want to live out here?" We'd say, 'Why not?'

"I like the place," Amundsen continued. "I camped and lived around there for years. They say it's dangerous to camp in the desert around there at night. I'd hear people moving through, crossers from Mexico, heading north to get work. They never bothered me."

George's apparent serenity and confidence seemed unusual. Manny made a mental note not to mention that to Reina, for fear of being reminded about the value of meditation, nonviolence, and the like. He made another mental note to double-check his handguns for function before he went out to Ajo.

"Who can I talk to that might know something about the crime scene in Ajo?" Manny asked.

"Go to the Coyote Howls Park," George said. "Ask for Bud Beck. He was a drug counselor in Ajo."

Manny wrote *Coyote Howls Park* on one page of a small black notebook. "Does Bud Beck have an email or a phone?"

"He does but I don't have it," George said. "He spends his winters at the Coyote Howls. He should be there."

"What can you tell me about Ajo?" Manny asked.

"Ajo means 'paint' in the Tohono O'odham language. They used a red ore pigment to paint their bodies. The Spanish mined silver there in the 1700's. We got Ajo in the Gadsden Purchase. It's an old copper mining town. The copper mines are shut down now. A lot of people from the north—snowbirds—stay in Ajo all winter long. There's quite a bit to do if you're retired. People volunteer for the Cabeza Prieta Wildlife Refuge. They have art shows. There's a good little library. You can take your laptop in there and recharge it. Lots of nice stuff in Ajo in the winter—old time fiddler's contests, and so on."

Manny bid goodbye to George and left La Indita for Jeff Goldman's office, where he found Reina tapping away at her computer.

"How was George?" she said, eyes on her monitor, not missing a beat on her keyboard.

"He gave me the name of a drug counselor who works out there," Manny said, "but I'll need to talk to Ajo law enforcement. Can we pull up a satellite map of Ajo?"

Reina clicked and tapped and a gray-green satellite map

appeared, parts of it running to a delicate dun color, soft as fur. Ridges and watercourses in the landscape, looking like a wrinkled paper, surrounded the grid of the town, but the central feature appeared as the emptied half shell of an oyster—the New Cornelia Copper Mine, almost as large as the town itself.

"That's their open pit mine," Reina said. "So very attractive."

"My father was a copper miner," Manny said.

"I know," Reina said. "It is what it is."

"Now," Manny said, "let's look for a drug counselor's place of residence, a guy named Beck. Beck's semi-retired, George says, and he lives at a place called The Coyote Howls Park."

"What?" Reina said. "The *Coyote Howls Park*?"

"I just write down what people tell me," Manny said, working hard at keeping a straight face.

"You knew it'd drive me nuts, Manny. How do you name something '*The Coyote Howls Park*'? That's heinous. I can't even think of a label for that kind of error." Reina muttered a pseudo-pagan curse that sounded like 'Ishtar's Balls' and navigated the map to the front entrance of The Coyote Howls Park, located on a narrow snake of desert two-lane near where State Route 86 banged up against State Route 85.

"There it is," she said, clicking a photo of a mailbox sporting some nicely faded block printing on its flanks. A wood or metal silhouette of a coyote sat on top of the mailbox, its head lifted, howling. Somebody had tied a red bandana around its neck. "Happy hunting," Reina said. She stood and looked into his eyes and held him and he looked back. "I get used to having you in town," Reina said. "See you when you get home."

When Manny had gone, Jeff Goldman called out softly from his office in the back of the building. "Did you tell him not to shoot anybody?"

Reina smiled a little grimly and tapped up another window on her monitor, covering the map of Ajo. "No, but I should have," she said.

Chapter Six

Manuel Aguilar drove west out of Tucson, on Ajo Road. He carried photographs of Lois and Donald Donahue, and a photograph of Lois's sister, Evelyn Antone. He carried a cell phone and a lap top, a camera, pens and notebooks, along with identification showing him to be a private investigator.

There was a lock box, chained in, underneath the seat of his Ford truck. He'd put his Colt 1911 in the lockbox, along with a .38 caliber backup gun. He did not expect to carry or to use his weapons. Manny was forty-three years old, a number close to the caliber of his primary carry weapon. His personal experience had taught him the obvious bad thing about gunfights: Somebody gets to go home. Somebody else does not. And the winner, if he's the good guy, only gets to keep what he already has.

Manny had just cleared the Tucson Mountains, heading west in open desert on the Ajo Highway, aka State Route 86, when his cell phone rang. He'd been watching the traffic and the roadside settlements on the fringe of metro Tucson. He read one more offering in a scattering of road signs: 'Don't Throw Jesus out with Your Christmas Decorations'—then he answered the cell phone.

"Manny, you'll be in Three Points in ten minutes, right?"

"Yes."

"I just talked to a guy I used to know—Coyote Bob—well, we don't call him Coyote Bob to his face—just Bob. He's got a Tohono O'Odham partner. He knows people who know people."

"I'll pull over," Manny said. The Ajo Highway was heavily traveled, regularly policed, and its shoulders were too narrow to safely bear motorists pulling over in pickup trucks. Manny caught a side road, drove about fifty feet down it, and told Reina to start talking.

"Bob says he'll meet you in front of the Three Points store. I told him what you look like."

"I like it better when you tell me what other people look like," Manny snapped.

"I kept it simple for both of you," Reina replied, "because you look like a cop, okay Manny? You look like a Flatfoot, The Heat, The Klingons, The Bulls, The Screws, The Buttons. Coyote Bob is harmless. Relax."

"If he's harmless why does he make it a point to notice people who look like cops?" Manny asked. "And another thing, who's the 'we' in 'We don't call him Coyote Bob to his face'?"

"Every woman who's ever known him calls him Coyote Bob because it's nicer than calling him 'Weasel Dick Bob,'" Reina said, her tone going slightly acerbic. "He's a painter and sculptor. He's smarter than he looks. He taught art for years at the TO high school in Sells. Dear old Coyote Bob still likes to smoke marijuana. Therefore, he is known to wet his pants ever so slightly when unexpectedly encountering big men who look like cops. By the way, he's a visual artist, so he'll look at you in a funny way. Just means he's analyzing your face as a composition."

"I like the weasel dick part of it," Manny said. "Do I have to call him by his street name or does he have a first and last name of record?"

"I'm sure you like this guy for the weasel dick part, Manny. I used to drink, remember? So one morning I wake up with Bob and a vicious hangover. I made sure that never happened again."

"How'd the hangover work out?" Manny asked, hoping to run a verbal nail file over Reina's nerves.

"The hangovers kept on for a few years until I realized they were somehow connected with my drinking. His name is Robert Ward. Tell him 'Hi' for me—and, as for you, Prince Charming, keep yourself in your pants when you're out there in Ajo. I've known you since high school, remember? It's not like you haven't had a few drunken one-nighters in your life. And I'm doing you one more favor." The favor was Coyote Bob's cell phone number and Manny punched it into his own phone before he spun his Ford truck around and eased back onto Highway 86.

***

The Three Points General Store lay behind a bulky aluminum ramada, painted blue and white and marked with Chevron logos. The ramada shaded a collection of fuel pumps set in the middle of a corner lot surrounded mostly by flat ground—Sonoran Desert ground, a kind of loose forest of mesquite trees, cactus, and other vegetation, which creates, for the uninitiated, the idea that there must be surface water, somewhere—and that rainfall must occur, pretty much as it does in other parts of the world. This idea, born by the site of plentiful vegetation, can kill, because these plants either draw water from deep underground or store it, as in the case of the giant Saguaro Cactus, in a thick, fibrous body—and none of these plants need the amount of water that any ordinary plant needs. Rain on this western desert will not fall for months on end and one sunny day will blend into another. If you have come as far as your body and this desert will let you, your life can end from thirst and heat a few feet behind the Three Points General Store. Here in the western desert, death wraps its shadow in the sun and appears, to the unwary, as just another nice day.

Manny pulled into the parking lot and swung his truck into an empty spot in front of the store, a low slung, flat roofed wooden building that went on forever, taking up most of one side of the lot on which it sat. He stepped out of his truck, slammed the creaking door, stepped sideways, and stood with his hands on one vertical side of his truck bed, scanning the parking lot. He saw, almost immediately, what appeared to be a pair of faded blue jeans somehow standing up by themselves. This image resolved itself into an ordinary human form when the man wearing the blue jeans straightened up, his top half encased in a denim shirt with snap buttons.

The man held a small bag in his hand and he appeared to be gesturing and speaking to thin air, and quite an audience of it at that, since he began turning to and fro in a semi-circle, addressing several directions at once. There was no one else in the parking lot. Manny watched the guy and waited for whatever was coming next.

A moment later, the man turned sideways, looking up, over his shoulder, at the big aluminum ramada which shaded the gas pumps. Manny looked in that direction and saw a raven, which had a good grip on the top of the ramada and was croaking happily as if it were addressing a crowd as well—which, indeed, it may have been, Manny realized, as he became aware of several other ravens hopping and croaking about the parking lot.

At the same time, the man caught sight of Manny and startled slightly, fear briefly clouding his pale eyes. Then the man waved and called out, "Manny?"

"Are you Robert Ward?" Manny asked.

The guy nodded his head. Manny stepped around the truck and shook hands with the man, a rather handsome Anglo who looked to be in his early fifties. The guy did look a little like a coyote, having a narrow face, a sizeable nose, and large eyes that bore an intense, oddly indifferent focus, as if he watched surfaces and saw faces as shapes. The bag he was holding turned out to be trail mix.

"Corvids," Bob said, as if that were supposed to mean something. "I like the word so I repeat it whenever I can. These guys are corvids," he went on, gesturing at the ravens, who hadn't given any indication of ever having been aware of the man, or the trail mix he'd offered them. "They run things out here."

Coyote Bob, odd bird that he was, had a Tohono O'odham girlfriend named Sasha. Sasha had some kind of administrative job at the TO nation's high school in Sells. Manny gave Bob a business card that identified Manny as an investigator for the Goldman law firm. Bob said he'd pass it on to Sasha and do what he could to help.

"Hope Wells told me you're with Reina," Bob said to Manny's back as Manny headed for his truck. "She left grill marks on the raw hamburger of my soul."

Manny turned and looked at Bob. Bob ducked his head and turned away, reaching into his sack of trail mix.

***

Manny wheeled his Ford truck out of the Three Points parking lot and back onto State Route 86. The sun was low in the west and light shone through shards of broken glass littering the desert on either side of the road, shards that were invisible when the sun was higher. Manny thought about the generations of driving drinkers it had taken to do this, throwing bottles and heading west into an Indian reservation roughly the size of Connecticut.

Topping a rise in the land, he began rolling through a series of signs, stating that federal officers were ahead. Speed limit warnings counted down to a stop sign where men and women stood, waiting and watching. They wore green uniforms accessorized with boots, baseball caps, and utility belts laden with weapons and equipment. The United States Border Patrol, operating under the Department of Homeland Security. An officer with a drug sniffing dog circled around the vehicles which were stopped at the checkpoint. If you were a winter visitor from some faraway place you were damn sure here now—in southern Arizona, where a multi-billion dollar a year business flourished in drug and human smuggling.

Having stated to the Border Patrol that he was an American, Manny kept going west, passing the Coyote Convenience Store, with the Wiwipul Du'ag Native American Arts Shop tucked away on one side of it. Then, on the south side of 86, Kitt Peak, 7,000 feet above the desert floor, sporting white astronomical observatories, looking like giant salt shakers poking up near the tip of the mountain's nose. He tapped a button on his dashboard and KOHN 91.9, Voice of the Tohono O'odham Nation, filled the cab of his truck with the voice of Elvis Presley singing *Love Me Tender*.

Passing through Sells, Manny saw ravens on the power poles. On down the highway, once again in uninhabited desert, he saw a brown bird with pointed wings and a slender tail flash out of the mesquite and fly across the road in front of him, seeming to watch him. Manny recognized it as a prairie falcon—*Halcon cafe* in Spanish. The sun went down and Manny drove for hours, into the night and its secrets, further west, running through a dim and endless landscape of rolling desert, until the road stopped at a T and his headlights drilled a reflective sign with arrows pointing south to Lukeville, a port of entry on the US-Mexico border, and north to Ajo, a town known to Manuel Aguilar only by its name. George Amundsen's former residence, the village of Why, located somewhere in the dark on the north side of Manny's truck, was not mentioned.

Manny drove the ten miles of desert and reached Ajo, feeling rather than seeing the terrain features on the outskirts of town. Something on his left, some kind of wall. Then something overhead that looked like an elevated train track. Seeing two white SUV's parked at Ajo's first real intersection brought things into focus—Pima County Sheriff's trucks, officers inside, waiting and watching. Maybe a police dog, too.

Manuel Aguilar wound his way through the deserted streets to a haphazard commercial strip on the north side of Ajo, where State Route 85 began to pick up again and disappear into the desert, heading north toward Phoenix.

A poisonous yellow bug light puked eternally on the sign for the Sundowner Motel. Manny paid and got a key to room number 13, finding two beds inside, at right angles to each other, and a kitchenette he wouldn't use. A chipped oval wall clock, hanging next to a flyswatter, told him it was 10:30 p.m. The Sundowner didn't have wireless.

He called Reina on his cell and let her know he was in for the night. He would visit Beck the next day and get the former drug counselor's take on the locals. Then he would ride with a Pima County Sheriff's officer, starting in midafternoon and rolling on into the night, the night being the time when things happened on Highway 85.

Manny had contacted his old captain at the Pima County Sheriff's Department to fix up the ride-along. He'd gotten clearance, but everybody knew who he was: a former Pima County Sheriff's Department, Criminal Investigations Division,

Homicide Detective—who'd gotten fired for a series of high profile shooting incidents—during which Manuel Aguilar had remained alive and wounded while an assortment of bad guys had ended up dead or wounded—but mostly dead.

Manny ate breakfast the next morning at Marcela's Café and Bakery and doubled back through Ajo, heading southeast. Near the edge of town, Well Road split to meet State Route 85, creating a small triangle with 85 as its base. A Ford Explorer and a Chevrolet Tahoe sat in the triangle—sheriff's trucks, white in color, and looking as if they hadn't moved since he'd passed them the night before.

Manny kept going, heading out of town for Why. He glanced at the overhead railway he'd passed the night before. It came to a dead end just over the highway and then a massive manmade wall of rock and gravel appeared to the right, on the west side of 85. A wall like the rumpled hide of a great animal, mostly reddish, shot with streaks of yellowish gravel sometimes running to chartreuse. The earth's rocky guts, turned out and dumped in the shape of a long loaf, a barrier, at least a hundred feet high. Ajo had been a copper mining town. This wall was a memento. They called it the Ajo mineral deposition.

He turned off 85 at Why and found the entrance to the Coyote Howls campground, marked by signs painted on boards, the paints going chalky from endless desert heat.

There was an office and a kind of clubhouse. Manny asked about a resident, Bud Beck. One person didn't know Beck, another person had heard of him. Yet another knew him but wasn't sure Beck hadn't taken off for Oregon. Still another said he knew about where Beck lived and told Manny to follow him in his truck.

The Coyote Howls RV Park and Campground, it turned out, was huge, covering multiple acres of flat desert, striated by dirt roads, only some of which were marked with signs. Trailer houses sat on the sides of these roads, reflecting no light, their dull aluminum skins bare or suffering under wan and ancient paints of the same corroded tints and textures as the Coyote Howls sign at the entrance. The trailers were spaced well apart, blending with the desert. Reina's friend George had given Manny the reasons why people came to this place, aside from the isolation and the peace that might come with it: the annual rent for a trailer space was five-hundred dollars. In advance.

Manny liked the place. New paint just made a shiny target out of a trailer house and the rent was low. The elemental, rogue male part of Manny, the piece of him that didn't like people and paying bills, lifted its head and sniffed the air. It fed on places like this. It squatted and ripped meat off bones with its teeth. Enough time in a trailer at the Coyote Howls and Manny would be both happy and unfit to live in ordinary society. If he didn't love Reina and PI work so much, he thought, he would buy a used trailer at the Coyote Howls and stay here.

The guide stopped his truck and pointed at a trailer, a corroded aluminum shell. Manny could see the profile of an older man through the trailer windows. The guy wore a brown fedora. Nobody would tell you to take your hat off in the house when you were at the Coyote Howls. The guy seemed to be doing nothing but wearing his hat and staring out the window.

"Bud's next door," the man said when Manny asked him.

Beck was an Anglo in his fifties. Manny introduced himself and told Beck that he'd gotten his name from George Amundsen. Beck told him to come inside.

Manny estimated Beck's height at five-foot-seven. Manny stood six-feet-two and the cramped interior of the trailer seemed to be gunning for him. Beck pointed at a chair by the door.

The living space of Beck's trailer was in keeping with the style of the Coyote Howls. A lap top sitting open on a sleeping pad, stacks of worn paperbacks. A small table piled with gadgets. Manny recognized a Leatherman tool, a 10-inch crescent wrench, spark plugs. The rest of the table was taken up with metal parts of unknown origin, except for the centerpiece, a coffee pot.

Beck, the drug counselor, wore a brown felt cowboy hat with a narrow brim. His eyes were likewise brown, kindly and keen, looking in an engaged way at the world from behind square rimmed glasses connected by a crossbar and colored in flat silver. He wore a forest green pullover with the words *Las Vegas* stitched in its middle. Underneath that, the edge of another pullover could be seen, a black one. He wore faded blue jeans of a comfortable cut. A chain on Beck's belt held keys and passed by a small, sheathed hunting knife as it looped behind him to a trucker's wallet in his back pocket.

Manny opened a notebook and asked Beck to tell him about the drug scene in Ajo.

"What are you investigating?" Beck asked.

"I'm investigating the murder of a young Tohono O'odham female. The victim may have had a drug connection in Ajo. I've never been to Ajo before. I need a general sense of the environment out here. Everything you can tell me will help me." Manny leaned forward slightly and poised his pen over his notebook.

Beck started talking. His voice was pleasant and beautifully pitched, betraying no tone of anger or tension, but he hadn't been asked for the good news about Ajo and the bad news was plentiful.

"I work with kids, so most of what I can tell you has to do with teenagers. For a start, we've got three different gangs in Ajo, with a hundred or more people in each gang. 'Thirteen' is here. You know about them?"

"I worked homicides for the Pima County Sheriff's Department," Manny said. "We'd get murderers acting alone, or in a group, or on behalf of another group—or gang. Murders are almost always about money, love, or drugs."

"Drug murders," Beck said. "The gold standard. I'll tell you what I know about the drug culture in Ajo. The majority of the local criminals here are Latinos and a lot of them are gangbangers—like 'Thirteen.' They make a gang sign by making a thumb-finger circle and holding up the other three fingers. They'll pronounce *diez y trez* as 'day-see-trez.' Anglos don't catch the connotation.

"Prior to and during the Mexican Revolution Pancho Villa and his men would come here to hide out," Beck went on, "and work in the mines. This was before Villa became a revolutionary figure. When the Mexican revolution came, these Villistas brought their families here, making Ajo a safe haven from the fighting, which was going on east of here. Pancho became a major revolutionary player and he may have done some good for Mexico, but he was also a mule thief and a killer. He went from bandit to revolutionary, like a lot of his men. Their descendants, so the story goes, make up the main bunch of local criminal families. In my experience, this town is tainted with the Villista personality style and lifestyle. They live in the spaces in between. They don't need to fit into the court system or legitimate American society. They have money. I've counseled generations of them, before they quit in grade school or dropped out of high school. There's an Ajo local here who works in the courts. She comes from this underground culture and she protects certain people who get DUI's, drug arrests, even burglary charges. As a result, these addicts never get the treatment they need. I understand you probably come at this from a law enforcement point of view, Manny. But to me, when addicts commit a crime, whether it's endangering lives by driving drunk or stealing to support a drug habit, I see an opportunity to help that drunk or that drugger change his life. An arrest interrupts the behavior. Follow that with court-ordered drug and alcohol counseling and you can bring people back to sanity." Beck leaned forward in his chair. "I've also counseled dozens of undocumented Mexicans who enter the court system—for alcohol offenses, mostly. A drug offense means deportation. I wondered why they never showed up for court mandated counseling. This probably isn't news to you because you're a detective but it took me awhile to realize they lived and worked under false names and that they had a completely different identity waiting for them in Mexico. Aside from that, a lot of them couldn't read. I've seen a grown man or two cry when he was taught to write his own name and managed to do it on his own."

Manny kept listening—and waiting. Reina didn't talk about it much, but she'd told him she was an alcoholic, a recovered alcoholic—somebody who'd been addicted and learned how to quit. He missed her already. He wanted her in her bedroom. He wanted to ball her. When he regained his focus, Beck was still talking.

"...I'll counsel the kids," Beck was saying. "Later on, I'll see their names in the Ajo Copper News, when they become adults and start getting arrested. I'll remember reading about their *grandfather's* arrests in the Copper News. You could pick up a copy. It'll help you with the local Ajo scene. When I started working here it cost thirty-five cents. I know a retiree in Ajo who works as a reporter for them. Do you want his name? " Beck uncrossed his legs, unlaced his fingers, and leaned forward, bracing his elbows on the arms of his chair.

"Yes," Manny said.

"His name's Bill Walker. You can look him up at the Copper News office in town." Beck went on talking about the local crime scene. "I was counseling a kid once, for alcohol and drug-related offenses," Beck said. "He was twelve years old. 'How much do you make a year?' he asked me. I told him I made about twenty-four thousand a year as a drug and alcohol counselor. The kid said 'I take my quad. I pick up these bundles out on the rez. I make seventeen-thousand dollars every time I do this. I do this twice a month.' I realized I couldn't point this kid in any positive direction. The kid did time later and now he's back in Ajo. Criminals with local family connections get a break in the courts. Some of the kids I've counseled seem to know the fix is in. They can't be convinced to get clean and sober, stop dealing drugs, or stay in school. They know they won't have to face real consequences as long they operate in Ajo. That's the general situation out here. What happened to the woman you say was murdered?"

"The woman was shot. Whoever did it left her body in her car and set the car on fire. The FBI and the Tohono O'odham Criminal Investigators went to the villages, talking to people around the case. Tohono O'odham CI's are good investigators. So far, they've come up empty. Knowing that and hearing from my informant made me want to look at Ajo."

"Anything else?"

Manny knew Beck was fishing and sensed Beck would have a reason. "Whoever did it cut her finger off to get her wedding ring," Manny said.

"Very few people will do that," Beck said.

Manny nodded, watching Beck, seeing a man getting ready to take a guess.

"I counseled a kid a few years ago—for drugs," Beck said. "He was known to torture animals. They caught him doing it when he was eight years old, then again when he was twelve, if I remember right. He'd be eighteen by now."

"What's his name?"

"Devin Woods."

Manny jotted down the name and looked up at Beck. "Can you tell me anything else about him?"

"He's an Anglo kid. He lived with his grandmother. Parents gone—probably druggers who left him with the grandmother. When you torture animals the word gets around and most of the other kids are wary of you, whether they're gangbangers or not. Not so much with Devin Woods. He's got a few friends. He hangs with some thugs. He speaks and understands some Spanish, like a lot of Anglo kids who grow up on the border. I'd check with the Pima County Sheriff's Department. They'll know him. And by the way," Beck said, "you didn't hear it from me."

Manny broke out his photographs, a short stack of 8x10's. Lois Donahue was on top. "This is a photo of the woman who was killed," he said. "Ever seen her in Ajo?"

Beck shook his head. Manny shuffled the photographs, showing Beck two images of Donald Donahue, one with the inevitable cowboy hat, one without. Beck shook his head again.
Evelyn Antone came up—the little sister—Jonas's caretaker, wearing her horn rimmed glasses.

Beck leaned back in his chair and nodded. "I've seen her in town," he said, "at the grocery store.

Chapter Seven

Manny drove out of the Coyote Howls and ran northwest on 85 to the intersection where he'd seen the sheriff's vehicles the night before. Once there, he turned north, up Well Road, to the Pima County Sheriff's Department and Corrections Facility, Ajo Station. For Manuel Aguilar, any new place was best seen through the eyes of local law enforcement—but, when it came to Ajo and the Pima County Sheriff's Department, he was a marked man, an outsider who'd once been a respected PCSD detective—before they'd fired him for being in one too many gunfights. He'd been lucky to be approved for a ride-along at all.

Once inside the sheriff's field station, Manny found himself looking through a heavy glass partition at a large office. The place had no smell, not even of cleaning fluid. A civilian sat facing him on the other side of the glass. Behind her, a coms guy, a dispatcher, sat in front of a console full of electronics. It looked like there was plenty of chatter going on, even though it was the middle of the afternoon.

Manny stated his business to the civilian and soon a sheriff's officer came through a thick metal side door. The guy was big and Manny could see he was all cop—large and deadly serious.

"Mr. Aguilar," the man said, "I'm Officer Tellez."

They shook on it.

"Do you have any weapons?" Tellez's voice was soft and he spoke with the cool neutrality of an on-duty law enforcement officer.

Manny knew a warning when he heard one. "I signed off on the rules when I signed up for the ride-along."

"Come in," Tellez said. He held the door open and let Manny pass. Manny could feel Tellez's eyes on his back of his shirt, searching for the imprint of a handgun. "Take the first door on the left. Lieutenant Davis wants to see you before we go out."

Manny found himself in a large office, one side of it taken up by the customary love-me wall full of plaques and trophies. A big desk sat front and center with a big man behind it.

The big man gestured at a chair in front of the desk. "Mr. Aguilar, have a seat."

Manny sat.

"What brings you out to Ajo?" the lieutenant asked.

Manny summarized the case—a murder on the rez, a defendant, Donald Donahue, and a trail that slipped out the west end of the rez and into Ajo. Manny didn't add that he'd just talked to Beck. Nor did he ask for any help. He decided to ease into that a little later, after these Ajo officers relaxed a little bit.

The lieutenant listened. "Good luck with it," he said, stiffly. "Take care of yourself while you're here. Officer Tellez will show you how to access an AR 15 rifle while you're riding along on his patrol. We all hope that you won't need it. I won't ask you if you brought any weapons with you to Ajo. I will tell you that we don't want to see you use them."

"I understand you, Lieutenant, but you can believe I won't hesitate to defend myself and I'm not ashamed of having done so in the past. Can I go on the ride-along now?"

"If you defend yourself—as you put it—out here, Mr. Aguilar," the lieutenant said, "your reputation will follow you into the courts—just as it has followed you here to the Ajo Station of the PCSD. Go on your ride-along."

***

Tellez was waiting just outside the lieutenant's door. "Go to the end of the hall and turn left," Tellez said.

Manny did as he was told, walking through a doorway at the end of the hall. There were desks, chairs, maps on the wall. Two of the chairs were occupied. One by an officer, the other by a prisoner with his hands cuffed behind his back—a clean, dark skinned man with curly gray hair, cut above collar length. Manny reflected that the guy looked almost upscale.

"Sit over there," Tellez said to Manny. He pointed to a chair behind a gray metal desk.

Manny sat, back to the wall, facing the room. He could see jail cells down a passageway that ran to the other side of the field station.

"I knew you guys wanted to see me," the prisoner said. "That's why I called you when I heard about the warrant. I ain't runnin' from nothin'."

It went on like that. The officer took the cuffs off the guy, still chatting with him.

After a while, the officer turned his head and called out toward the jail side. "Need an escort with a Folger Adam."

A jailer appeared with a key the size of a pancake turner, a key made by the Folger Adam company. The jailer took the prisoner away.

Tellez stood in the middle of the room and watched the prisoner and the jailer walk out. "Frequent flyer," Tellez said, nodding at the prisoner's back. "He was Army Airborne before he logged thirty years on alcohol and methamphetamine. He'll be on video court this weekend, out of Tucson. If he's convicted of a felony, he'll be transported to Tucson to serve his time. If it's a misdemeanor, he'll serve it here in our jail." Tellez turned toward Manny. "I'm supposed to give ride-alongs an orientation. I know you're familiar with most of the equipment we use." Tellez pointed at a computer screen filled with colored columns. "ACIJIS."

Manny nodded. "Statewide criminal record lookup."

"Spillman?"

"In-house network," Manny said.

Tellez reached in his pocket and held up a booklet.

"Codes," Manny said.

Tellez started patting the gear on his belt. "Taser. Pepper spray—like hotsauce on your face. Baton. Radio with an earpiece so no one else can hear you. Two pairs of handcuffs. Gloves, flat badge. Glock 22 in .40 Smith with spare magazines. Fifteen cartridges in each magazine."

Manny nodded.

Tellez turned and pointed across the room at a row of round shapes sitting on a table, black bags with gray stripes. "Helmet bags. At PCSD, Ajo, we're all quad certified. Border Patrol has an all-terrain vehicle unit. Those guys usually ride pretty deep. They use an LEO model of quad. It's got a cargo area for supplies, equipment and dead bodies. We keep a radio on the Border Patrol frequency."

"How far are we from the border?" Manny asked.

"Thirty-eight miles," Tellez said. "Are you ready to go?"

Manny nodded.

"If you want to stop for dinner later on, we can do that," Tellez said. "I eat before my shift. You can't see it happen if you're not in your vehicle."

"No problem," Manny said.

They left the building through a side door. Tellez walked a few feet to an SUV and popped the hatchback. Manny stood and watched while Tellez gave a running inventory of the equipment.

"We drive Ford Expeditions and Chevy Tahoes," Tellez said. "We carry extra water, a spike kit, a hydration pack, a PPE bag— Personal Protection Equipment. We've got a chemical warfare suit and a riot helmet in the PPE bag. We've got extra gloves. We've got a fire extinguisher." Tellez shut the hatchback, moved to the passenger door of the truck, unlocked it and held it open. Manny got in. Tellez came in on the driver's side, cranked the engine, and tapped buttons on a computer which sat between them. Color coded columns appeared on the screen.

"Mobile data computer," Tellez said, "made by Tough Books. It'll take a lot of abuse. You've used them." He tapped a section of the screen, "GPS."

A black rifle stood muzzle up, secured in a metal gun rack by an electronic lock. "AR-15 with a twenty-round round magazine. Eighteen rounds loaded." Tellez pointed at a toggle switch. "If you need the AR, flip that switch," he said.

Tellez tested his lightbar and siren. They rolled out and headed south to the triangle at the bottom of Well Road. Tellez waved at an officer parked in the triangle. The officer waved back with his free hand. His other hand held a radar gun. Tellez turned right, heading into town. Manny could see Ajo's Camelback Mountain ahead, which stood over Ajo like a miniature of the Corcovado in Rio de Janerio. A big white "A," made from whitewashed rocks, stood partway up the mountain. Instead of Rio's Christ figure with its arms outstretched, a white Christian cross stood at the very top. In this desert, Manny thought, people needed all the help they could get.

Reina had once made a point of telling Manny, in an argument about illegal immigration, that out here in the western Arizona deserts the ground temperature could hit 130 degrees.

"Do you find bodies in the desert around here?" Manny asked.

"A few dozen a year," Tellez said. "Summer—that's the dead body season. We have a storage facility at the station and a freezer locker for body parts. I'll show them to you when we get back."

Tellez began a running commentary on the major business of the Pima County Sheriff's Ajo Station. "Smugglers will run north to south, up and down Arizona State Route 85," Tellez said. "Drugs and illegals go north on 85. Money and guns go south. You can legally have up to ten-thousand in cash when you cross the border. A few months ago we seized seventy-thousand dollars in one car. We've seized tons of marijuana in the Ajo area. At Lukeville, the port of entry, the border town, big busts are routine."

"What about the rez?" Manny asked.

"Sometimes smugglers run east-west, through the rez on State Route 86. Recently, they've set up another Border Patrol checkpoint south of town, below the turnoff to 86. That's stopped the free ride on 86 from east to west through the reservation. Before they set up that checkpoint anybody could come up from the border, turn east on 86, and take a side road north through the nation. Smugglers still come in on the reservation itself, though.

"Vehicles that come south on 85 will stop at a certain

milepost. They'll start honking and the UDA's —undocumented aliens —will come out of the desert and throw the dope in the vehicle—or, if it's human smuggling, they'll jump in themselves. They use rest stops, too. They'll key on lights on towers to help them navigate. If we see a lone driver coming through town and he's got a dozen burritos in the front seat and some gallon jugs of water we know he's down here to do a pickup and take some people back up to Phoenix." Tellez paused, listening to radio traffic.

"What kind of ID do these people carry?" Manny asked.

Tellez waited until the chatter on the radio went quiet. "UDA's have a Mexican voter ID card," he said. "That's the most common type of ID. Border Patrol makes a permanent record of every voter ID card they find on anybody."

"Do these runners and smugglers drive any special kind of vehicle?"

"Smugglers tend to use older four-wheel drives—any kind of truck or large SUV. We also key in on beaters, early Nineties cars. Nobody wants to lose a nice vehicle. We don't profile people but we do profile vehicles. Anybody could be a smuggler—Americans with businesses in Rocky Point, for example. If we see a nice truck heading south that looks like it's been driven off road, we're likely to stop it, too.

"The cartels also use a trick that's got them by us before. They'll steal a big four wheel drive in Phoenix. They like Dodge Rams and the older Ford F250's. The newer Fords have the chip key. They'll swap the plates with another truck that's the same color and model. Sometimes they make it into Mexico before we get them. Meanwhile, a law abiding citizen starts the drive to work in a truck with stolen plates and finds himself in a felony stop situation with Phoenix area law enforcement—guns pointed at him. All he can do is have nothing in his hands and keep his hands in sight. Not making any sudden moves is a great idea, too." Tellez glanced at Manny. "But you know that part of it," he said.

***

They rode for hours, cruising up and down Ajo's main drag, running south of town past the massive Ajo mineral deposition. When they passed by the Sheriff's station again Tellez pointed at a ridge a couple hundred yards east of the station.

"See how the trees are trimmed up on that ridge? We did that after we found out the smugglers had spotters camped up there, eating food out of cans and watching the station. They know when we change shifts. Spotters will sit up on high ground all over southern Arizona and use throwaway cell phones to let smugglers on the ground know when it's safe to move. I've heard estimates that the cartels have as many as two-hundred spotters working across the state. They've even built portable cell phone towers. They run them with car batteries. We've done operations with other units to take drug scouts off mountain tops. I've seen spotters with a half-dozen disposable cell phones on them. Some spotters stay out for weeks. Other smugglers resupply them with food and water." Tellez spun the truck around and headed back towards the triangle at the base of town.

"What about murder?" Manny asked. "Ever catch anybody who'd done a murder in the US and was running for the border?"

"Once or twice," Tellez said. "Not since I've been here, though. I think LAPD holds the record on that. Back in the Eighties, they had over two-hundred homicides where they had enough on the suspect to issue an arrest warrant. The perps were mostly Mexican nationals and LAPD believed they were hiding in Mexico. That's when they started working close up with Mexican police on homicides."

Tellez spun the truck around again and cruised north, nearly clearing the north end of Ajo before pulling off on a side road and spinning around to face highway 85.

Tellez pointed off to the north, to miles of flat desert with mountains in the distance on either horizon. "That's all the Goldwater Bombing Range," he said. "When they do live fire exercises at night they'll be colored flares in the air and bombs going off. You can hear the automatic cannons on the A-10

Warthogs out of the airbase in Tucson. They fire rounds about the size of a longneck beer bottle at 3,900 per minute. They're all incendiary—armor piercing rounds mixed with high explosive rounds. From far away it looks like a bed of hot coals on the ground and it's thousands of rounds hitting at the same time.

"Word is, a truck full of dope got tagged out on the Goldwater one time on a night fire exercise. A bomb fell on the cab and didn't detonate. It might have been a practice bomb, designed to pop some smoke to mark the spot where it hit. Two dead Mexican Nationals were in the truck cab and a few hundred pounds of pot was in the back. These guys were running through the desert with their lights off, headed for Phoenix."

***

The sun was nearly down when they pulled up at the triangle. Tellez pointed up at Ajo's guardian mountain, the Camelback. "When you see those hills start to turn pink things start happening. Evil loves darkness. What are you looking for in Ajo?"

Manny gave Tellez the facts around Lois Donahue's murder and broke out the photographs of the Donahues and the little sister, Evelyn Antone.

As Beck had done before him, Tellez pointed not at Lois but at Evelyn Antone's picture. "I've seen her here. I remember running her plate. It didn't turn up anything. Just an FYI, if you never worked the TO nation when you were with PCSD—we have jurisdiction on Natives here in Ajo, but not on the rez. We do have jurisdiction over non-Natives on the rez."

Manny put the photographs away. Tellez watched a car drive by. The driver's hands were glued to the steering wheel in a white-knuckle ten-two position. Tellez cranked up his truck and fell in behind the motorist, trailing him through town while running the license plate on the computer. The motorist made no mistakes and the computer check came back negative. Tellez parked off Highway 85 on the north side of town and waited.

It was time for Manny ask about Devin Woods. "I got the

48

name of a local kid who was known to torture animals," Manny said. "The guy is old enough to have a driver's license. I understand he's a drugger—Devin Woods. I thought he might be the kind of guy who would cut off a finger to get a ring."

"We know about him," Tellez said. "He's got friends who are known dopers and dealers. I could show you where he lives."

Tellez rolled back onto State Route 85 and drove back into town. He was signaling for a left turn when a car passed in the opposite direction. Tellez spun around and followed the car. "I'll show you Devin Woods's house later. This guy in the Camaro is a local dealer."

***

It was after sundown before the dealer screwed up. He did a left turn without signaling and drove halfway over a dividing line in the road before correcting his steering. Tellez turned on the flashing lights, got the car stopped, and called in a sniff dog. Manny watched from the passenger seat of Tellez's SUV while a K9 officer let a leashed and eager Belgian Malinois go over the Camaro. The dog alerted on the storage compartment in the driver's side door and the officers checked it. Dope had been in that side pocket but it wasn't there now. If the dealer had anything, his girlfriend, standing by him, lit by the police lights, was packing it someplace where the sun didn't shine. Good sniff dog or no, this particular little Ajo dealer had beat the law—this time, anyway.

Tellez and the dealer had been making small talk while the dog did its run. Tellez and the K9 officer bade the kid a good night and let him go.

"Peace out!" the kid said, on his way back to the Camaro.

Tellez got back in the truck, shut the door, and buckled up. "I'll show you where Devin Woods lives."

They cruised across town, angled through a few streets, and came up on a nondescript white frame house trimmed in green. All the lights were on, the front door was open, and the music was playing loud. Tellez's radio came alive, requesting a response to a noise disturbance at that address.

"Perfect timing," Tellez said, after he'd let the coms guy know he was already on the site of the disturbance. "That's Devin Woods. Stay here."

Tellez got out of the truck, leaving the door slightly ajar. His eyes were focused on a man standing in the front yard of the house. Manny quietly unlocked the door on his side of the truck. If anything went wrong, common sense would dictate the option of mobility, whether that meant shoot, run, or both.

Manny was unable to hear most of Tellez's conversation with Devin. It was the usual perp and cop pantomime. It wasn't long before Manny saw Tellez point at something on the white plastic lawn chair Devin had blocked with his body as Tellez approached. A little more conversation and then Tellez hooked up Devin with a set of handcuffs and put him in the back seat of the SUV. The lad sulked all the way back to the PCSD Ajo complex.

Devin remained rebellious once he'd been unloaded and put in a chair. He was a skinny kid with spooky gray eyes and a few telltale tweaker sores on his cheeks. Tellez and another officer verbally double-teamed Devin about the bag of white powder Tellez had noticed on his lawn chair. Devin wouldn't tell them what it was or how he got it. The officers brought in the sniff dog. The dog alerted on the powder, indicating methamphetamine. The officers put the baggie aside to await the kind attention of a DRE, a Drug Recognition Expert, who would not be long in coming. Then, before putting Devin himself aside—in a jail cell—the officers asked him a few of Manny's questions, allowing Manny to sit in.

Devin looked right at Manny when Tellez put the photograph of Lois Donahue in front of him and asked if he knew her. Devin stuck his chest out and said hell no. Same reaction with Evelyn Antone and Donald Donahue. Then it was just a matter of a jailer with a Folger Adam appearing and taking Devin across the station to the cells.

Manny watched him being led off, pondering Devin's

haircut—a haystack piled on the kid's head, making him resemble a Japanese anime character—not that Manny had ever seen an ignorant small town tweaker represented as a Japanese anime character. Manny tried to remember in what decade—or on what planet—that haircut had been workable in anything besides cartoons. Reina, of course, would know. Manny reflected that a stylish lad like Devin Woods would certainly have a Facebook page. He made a mental note to check it the next day, before he left Ajo. He made a second mental note to look up Bill Walker, the retiree who wrote articles for the local paper.

Chapter Eight

Manny checked out of the Sundowner Motel the next morning and drove to the Ajo town plaza, a place with a park like an old fashioned keyhole, a rectangular shape furnished with a green lawn and palm trees. The west end of the park, the end that sat on Ajo's main drag, was rounded. The other end, where the modest Ajo Tower stood, was flat. Businesses lined two sides of the plaza. Manny got coffee and drank it at a sidewalk table.

He drove around the plaza to the Ajo library, fired up his laptop, and found an entry on Devin Woods's Facebook page made the day of Lois Donovan's death. Devin was using Facebook to call the Tohono O'odham police by a few ugly names on the day Lois Donohue was killed. He'd been passing through the rez on his way to Tucson and he'd gotten a speeding ticket near Sells. Devin Woods made no dark hints about harming anyone. Nor did he make any Satanic references, or post any pictures of himself holding an assault rifle or sticking up his middle finger, or making the horned devil sign, or displaying any of the painfully clichéd and archaic cultural signals put forth by people who didn't read books or apply any real discernment to contemporary online media. Nor did he make any stupid gang signs, like the thumb and finger circle of *Diez y Tres*, MS-13, the Salvadoran gang Bud Beck knew to be in Ajo. Still, Manny liked it. It put Devin Woods, apparent methamphetamine enthusiast and sometime animal torturer, on the rez the day Lois died. It also put Devin on the way to Tucson, which was out of his way. Ajo residents shopped in Casa Grande or Phoenix—especially metropolitan Phoenix, with a population in the millions. Not Tucson. Devin must have had a reason to drive all the way there on the day Lois died.

Manny left the library, took a seat in his truck and called the Tohono O'Odham Police. They wanted a faxed request on letterhead for any information about Devin Woods getting any speeding tickets on any day. Manny called Reina and asked her to fax said request. He told her it probably wouldn't do any good, coming from the Goldman Law Firm, and, if it didn't, he'd try something else.

"If the TO police don't respond I'll let Jeff know," Reina said. "Maybe one of the investigating feds will talk to us. And don't forget Coyote Bob. Call him while you're out there. I'll tell Jeff about Devin Woods."

***

Manny dropped by the Ajo Copper News office, a pleasant place, consisting of a little bookstore and stationers downstairs with newspaper offices upstairs.

A man wearing a pair of half glasses on his nose sat behind a desk in the corner. "Can I help you?"

"I'm looking for William Walker," Manny said.

"He's over at the Curley School," the man said. "He'll be there for an hour. He just left. Anything I can help you with?"

Why not, Manny thought. The guy looked smart and observant. Manny got out his badge case and identified himself.

"Chuck Dacey," the man said. He stood and shook Manny's hand.

"I'd like to show you some photos," Manny said.

Dacey paused over the photograph of Evelyn Antone. "Her," he said, pointing. "She was in here, asking for something."

***

Manny headed out for the Curley School. Doing so involved driving up Esparanza Avenue while staring at a massive piece of architecture done in Spanish Colonial Revival style—the Curley School, built in 1919. The ornate, muscular design, bought with piles of money from copper mining, must have impressed students, Manny thought, even before they got in the door. The place seemed to promise both a bright future through education and a real bad present if a kid screwed up inside the building—but kids hadn't gone to school there for years. Curley School was now an arts complex, complete with what were being called artisan apartments.

Manny parked and went into a gallery tucked in on the north side of the complex. He walked through an airy room with a high ceiling, moving past sculptures and glancing at paintings on the walls. The smiling couple sitting together at the desk in the back of the room pointed at a white man who wore crisp casual clothing done in pastels. The man was scribbling in a narrow notebook which appeared to Manny as unusually long—a relic—a reporter's notebook. When the man stopped writing and lifted his head, still looking at the painting, Manny stepped in, introduced himself, and dropped Beck's name.

William Walker shook Manny's hand and smiled. Walker had a good amount of silvery hair on his head, well-trimmed at the sides and back. His hazel eyes were narrow, holding soft flecks of gold and green. He was a fit old man, Manny noticed, and he carried himself well.

"Wait for me outside, Manny," Walker said, after Manny had stated his specific business, "I won't be more than a minute." Walker headed for the two art show caretakers at the back of the room.

***

"So Bud Beck told you I might know some stories about Ajo," Walker said, when he had joined Manny outside. "I don't know as much as he thinks I do. I report on community events. I sell sunshine, so to speak, and that suits me fine." The gold and green in Walker's eyes warmed up a few degrees and his thin lips curled up in a wispy grin. "I do write up some of the stories about drug seizures. I know the drugs go through Ajo on 85 and that there are locals involved. I heard there's supposed to be thirty-some undercover DEA agents working in Ajo. I've never heard of them arresting anybody. They're supposed to be building cases."

Walker chuckled. "But Beck's right. We publish the Sheriff's Log in the Ajo Copper News and ninety percent of the entries in that log involve narcotics, paraphernalia, and smugglers. I'll keep you in mind when I'm doing my work and I'll let you know if I come across anything."

Bill Walker had never heard of Devin Woods, the haystack-headed animal torturer. He shook his head when Manny showed him the mugshot of Evelyn Antone in her little black retro eyeglasses. Bill Walker had never seen Manny's cowboy client, Donald Donahue, or Donny's wife Lois, now deceased. Walker waved a good bye and strode off down Esperanza Avenue toward the plaza at the center of town.

***

There was something about William Walker, something wasn't right. He had a kind of military bearing, but not quite. An old cop's affect, but not quite. He said he'd retired in Ajo but Manny couldn't see an intense guy like Walker, even if he was older, being satisfied with the pace of life there. Manny became aware that something was pushing him to look at Walker. Manny knew that if he pushed the feeling away it would come back. And it would bring reinforcements—in the form of hallucinations of his deceased Yaqui grandmother—if they were hallucinations, and not some other kind of reality. Either way, Manny didn't want to see his grandmother. He decided to check Walker out and hope nothing came up because, if it did, the feeling would bore in on him, and his grandmother would drive him nuts. She would help him, maybe—probably, but she would definitely drive him nuts.

It was noon now and the white buildings of Ajo glowed in still and shadowless light. From the high ground by the Curley School Manny watched the desert hills that rose up on the east side of town, frozen in their tawny banality, bone dry and the color of a cougar's skin. No breeze blew. A dust devil started up by the high school below the hills, near the triangle of roads where the white sheriffs' trucks sat. The devil made a funnel of brown dirt and dotted it with candy wrappers and wrinkled pages of discarded homework assignments. Manny made a mental bet with no one in particular that the dust devil was the lost spirit of a high school dropout. It was time to take the long road back to Tucson.

At the triangle at the bottom of town Manny pulled his truck up alongside Officer Tellez's, taking care to come in slow and make sure Tellez saw him and knew who he was. They rolled down their respective car windows.

"Devin Woods put a post on Facebook saying he got a speeding ticket on the TO Nation the day of Lois Donahue's murder," Manny said.

Tellez almost smiled. "I'll take a look at that," he said. "The DRE verified meth in Devin's baggie. Devin had his moment in video court this morning. He's going to be with us for some time to come."

"Do you know any TO patrol officers I could talk to about it?"

Tellez didn't know anybody on the rez. They gave each other a wave and Manny headed southeast on Highway 85.

When Highway 86 came up at the Y, Manny turned left, heading east. He had just passed the green highway sign marking the turnoff for Gu Vo when he remembered Coyote Bob and Bob's Tohono O'odham girlfriend, Sasha. He kept driving until he was clear of Gu Vo. The westernmost settlement on the rez, lying south of Highway 86 near the high, rough wilds of the Ajo Mountains, Gu Vo was a natural habitat for smugglers. Green and white Border Patrol trucks sat just off 85 at the Gu Vo turnoff. Manny remembered seeing them when he'd come through at night. If anybody stopped for any reason the Border Patrol would drive up and check it out. It had happened to Manny before. He'd barely had time to zip his pants. Reina would be disgusted with Homeland Security's insistence on watching everybody who came and went from Gu Vo. So, doubtless, were its inhabitants.

Coyote Bob answered his phone and said he'd call Manny back when and if he could get his girlfriend Sasha to get anything out of the TO Police about Devin Woods's traffic ticket. Manny cranked up the rez radio station and kept driving.

***

Back in Tucson, Manny pushed the heavy door open, felt the draft of warm air in Goldman's white bungalow, stepped behind Reina's desk and grabbed her as she stood and put herself close into his arms. Kisses and nose rubbing followed.

Goldman, sitting in his back office and reading a file, had heard the door and the slight rustling noises and the silence that followed. He knew his employees like a mother knows her two-year old. Quiet meant bad. Manny and Reina might jump each other on the desk. He cleared his throat and kept reading. He knew that usually did it.

Manny and Reina broke apart. She put a hand in the middle of his chest and they looked each other in the eye and together they whispered, "Tonight."

Goldman, still in his office, having traveled a distance of six paragraphs since he'd cleared his throat, didn't hear the word but heard the whisper. In response, he banged a glass paperweight on his desk.

"We're fine," Reina said, in the direction of Goldman's office. "Thank you, Jeff. Please don't further abuse your Tom Philabaum glass paperweight. We're going to work now." She sat at her keyboard and looked up at Manny. "What do you need to know?"

Manny handed her Bud Beck's business card and watched her run her fingers over the keyboard for a while.

"Donald 'Bud' Beck," Reina said. "He's been a certified substance abuse counselor for fifteen years. Bud's got a couple of drug arrests from way back when. Looks like Beck's father was an inmate in the Washington State Penitentiary in Walla Walla. The father died in 1990. Bud Beck's a wounded healer, Manny."

"Sounds like an arrested healer to me," Manny said.

"Yeah, sure, Mr. drug warrior," Reina said. "I'm giving you the drug wars lecture tonight and you can listen to it from your cold little spot on the couch. Who's next?"

William Walker was fairly easy to find, despite having a

common name. The old reporter had bylines on a number of American newspaper stories, most of them originating out of Latin America. He'd graduated from the University of Virginia in 1964. No criminal record. Manny made a mental note that William Walker would almost certainly speak Spanish.

"Devin Woods is next," Manny said.

Reina shook her head. "He's got no record I can get into. He just turned eighteen. I've got nothing on that traffic ticket."

"It puts him on the rez the day Lois was killed," Manny said.

Jeff Goldman called out from his office. "Did you fax that request to the TO police?"

"I did, Jeff," Reina called back.

Manny heard a set of chair wheels rake a wooden floor and then Jeff appeared, framed in the door of his office. Lean, six feet tall, with a blade for a nose and dark brown eyes that betrayed a certain warmth and earnestness, Goldman's energy and ethics had earned him some respect among his more intelligent and ethical opponents in the prosecutorial legal system—but little cooperation. Goldman, after all, was the guy wearing the black hat.

 "Manny, were you able to tell PCSD in Ajo to take a look at Devin Woods?"

Manny nodded as he began to throttle his ringing cell phone into silence, then realized it was Coyote Bob calling and put his cell on speaker.

"Uh, Sasha did her magic," Bob mumbled. "She knows one of the women at the tribal police station, uh, in Sells, and Sasha says to tell you that the woman is faxing you a copy of Devin Woods's traffic ticket."

"Did she ask the officer for any additional information about Woods?" Manny asked.

"No, she can't do that, she said."

Manny thanked Bob and pressed the end button on his phone.

"Officer Tellez at PCSD Ajo Station will take a look at Devin Woods for Lois's murder," Manny told Goldman.

"Good, keep me advised," Goldman said. He stepped over to the office coatrack and threw on his jacket. "Let's call it a day."

***

Manny and Reina ripped each other's clothes off as soon they got to her house, scandalizing and outraging the cat and the dog, who had been counting on a timely dinner and more attention than they were given upon the return of their master and mistress.

Everybody got fed, eventually, and Manny and Reina found themselves back in bed a few hours later, having lavished attention on the cat and dog and having watched the local news, for what that was worth. Reina lit a candle, lay down beside Manny, and they started over again. When the two of them nestled in serious afterglow, Reina decided it was time to gently nudge her beloved hardnosed detective boyfriend into the sunshine of accepting the legalization approach to drugs, rather than the law enforcement approach.

"Remember when you called that Beck guy an arrested healer, Manny?" she said.

"You think you made love to me so now I'm relaxed and I'll listen to you," Manny said.

"Uh-huh." Reina ran a delicate caress over his nether regions.

"People use drugs, Reina," Manny said, a post-coital surge of aggression blooming in his bloodstream. "Getting arrested is the only thing that stops some people before they kill themselves with drugs—or before they kill somebody else. The fear of getting arrested is the only thing that keeps some other people from trying drugs. Drug counselors will tell you that—drug counselors who get in the faces of drug addicts and say *Look, you did this to yourself. You got in it and you can get out of it.* You told me you were an alcoholic, Reina. You beat it," Manny got up on one elbow and looked down at Reina. "Right?"

Reina got up on one elbow and looked Manny in the eye. "I can tell it's going to be an up on our elbows kind of night, Manny," she said, giving him a feline smirk. "I didn't get sober by myself. I couldn't have done it by myself, but never mind."

She fixed him with a compassionate and level look and started her lecture. "Here's the deal Manny. The drug treatment community itself is divided about the legal approach versus the medical approach. One way of presenting the medical model is telling a drunk, just for instance, that his brain didn't produce enough serotonin so he used alcohol as the sedative-hypnotic drug that it is and got hooked—addicted. The American Medical Association recognizes alcoholism as a disease, like other types of drug addiction—that's been their position for years. The disease model takes the responsibility off the addict and puts it on the disease. If you can understand you have a disease, you can get help. It's like having a broken arm. If I told you that you had a broken arm, would you let me help you?"

Manny shook his head.

"Yes you would, you jerk" Reina said. "But there's more."

"There's always more with you," Manny muttered.

"So why can't you be thankful? Here's the more part. Drug counselors themselves have to buy into—or at least represent the argument—that drugs are bad, in any amount, just because they're illegal, and if you take them, there's something wrong with you. This pays for the drug counselor's livelihood, but it creates a response in the user—to defy a system that's obviously hypocritical. The society that pushes alcohol and nicotine is the same society that jails you for smoking a joint and then puts a little drug counselor on your ass to shake his finger at you."

Manny didn't answer. He absently put a gentle hand between her thighs. She gently pushed the gentle hand away.

"Incarceration isn't treatment," Reina said. "It doesn't teach addicts coping skills, it doesn't show them what they're trying to mask by getting high, and it doesn't link them to resources. It's just punishment. Punishment for them and everyone around them—spouses, kids, parents—and these people are more prone to becoming dependent on society, rather than on themselves, because they come out of jail broke and, if they were convicted of a felony, unable to get a job."

Manny stared at empty space. His eyes had darkened. "You can't expect me to care if a drugger gets arrested. I work with you and Goldman and I do investigations to help defend people who've been arrested for drugs—that's part of my job. It's a legal system. I work in it. But there's information everywhere about drugs. Methamphetamine. It's a poison. Even the stupidest user knows that. Ask Devin Woods out there in Ajo. He knows—and he's real stupid. There are all kinds of drunks and drug addicts who will never quit. They don't want to. What do we do with them? Pay their medical bills? Buy them a house so they can lie around and use drugs?"

Reina settled into the argument, using her indoor voice, and an additional dose of humility and reason. "If we changed our approach we could stop a lot more addiction than we do now. And there's also a social context, a poverty context, which has to be addressed. But yes, we can't stop some people from being addicts and the social costs hurt society, Manny. But who really cares if somebody wastes their life doing drugs? Does that hurt more than criminalizing users and empowering drug cartels? Will it cost us more tax dollars if we don't have to drop twenty-five or thirty grand a year on keeping people in prison for having or selling drugs? A lot of those young guys come out of prison all hooked up with other criminals and itching to do crime on a level they'd never do if they hadn't got a prison education in being a vicious creep.

"Why pay taxes so the federal courts can prosecute smuggling cases? The feds make the big bucks and they get great retirement benefits—our tax dollar pays for that. And what about the banks? They launder the billions the cartels shove at them. Check it on the internet anytime you like. Read *El País*, or read the Mexican papers—you read Spanish. What to do about the social costs? How about children of incarcerated parents? Put all that private prison money and all that DEA and federal court money into taking care of kids whose parents are too wrecked on drugs to raise them. What would you rather do, take care of a kid or pay a cop to kick down doors? And let me ask you this: what's less expensive? Caretakers of children get way less money than federal judges who sentence people to expensive federal prisons."

"I've never seen a criminal who didn't use drugs, Reina," Manny said.

"Yeah, Manny," Reina replied, "criminals use drugs but not all people who use drugs are criminals. The only way to stop it is to take the money out of it. Jeff would welcome an end to the drug wars. A criminal defense attorney, especially one as good as Jeff, has human nature on his side. People commit crimes for drugs, money, and love—and that's not me saying it—you guys say that—you cops. Take away drugs and Jeff will still be in business. How would Jeff end the drug wars? I can tell you. He'd legalize and tax marijuana and treat drug addiction as a public health issue, not a crime."

"Reina, I've heard it from you and Jeff before," Manny said.

"That's because it's true," Reina said.

"I'm going to keep doing investigations," Manny said, in measured tones, "and not worry about it. And if I see a law enforcement officer make a drug arrest I will be fine with that because drugs, Reina, are illegal—and some drugs are pure poison, especially meth. So let's drop it."

Reina wasn't ready to drop it. She massaged the shoulder of the arm she was leaning on and fixed Manny with a cage fighter's stare. "Marijuana has proven medical uses but US authorities won't fund research in this country. According to the federal government, marijuana is a Schedule I drug, with no known medical uses. That's crazy. It's medical-legal or just plain legal and taxable in what, twenty states, and the feds still bust people for it? But marijuana is still a felony in Arizona, so no problem there, right? Nothing stopping our state from remaining a national embarrassment."

"Dammit, Reina," Manny said, "do you ever relax? Just take it easy?"

"I'll be mellow when I'm dead," Reina said. "Police corruption and trucking in drugs from Mexico under the guise of the NAFTA agreements isn't on the public docket. Americans don't hear about American cops working for Mexican cartels. Americans don't think it goes on all the time. Most people have never heard of Nuevo Laredo, Mexico. Over eight-thousand trucks go through that port every day—straight into Texas. NAFTA—and would you like some drugs with that, America?"

"You're turning this into a long, long night, Reina," Manny said.

Reina ignored him. "Joe Citizen doesn't even know the Mexican cartels live in our country," she continued. "They're all over our national forests, growing marijuana. They're extorting peaceful American marijuana dealers and taking over their operations. They're kidnapping migrants. They run cocaine from Columbia and they cook so much meth they need to import their raw materials from China. The Mexicans are ruining their country and they're ruining ours—and our federal government likes that, of course, because it keeps the drug wars going—"

Manny stared into a corner of the bedroom. "I know all this," he said.

"Just hear me out," Reina said. "I know you well enough to know there's some of it you don't know. Presidents of Latin American countries call for drug decriminalization—and, these days, a lot of them aren't even waiting until after they retire. And last but far from least, according the best casualty estimates in the Mexican cartel wars, Mexico has around 103,000 dead people—and a lot of them are innocents, caught in a spray of bullets—pregnant women, kids washing car windows. And the DEA is going to stop this? All they do is shoot people up in Latin America. They're even in Africa."

"Reina, that's not all the DEA does," Manny said. "There are a lot of DEA guys out there doing the best they can. They're professional law enforcement. Jeff will tell you that. They don't lie in court. They take big risks to do their job. Who told you they shoot people in Latin America? They work with the drug enforcement agencies in those countries as advisers. They don't shoot people themselves."

"That's not what I've read," Reina said. "Sometimes the DEA does its own shooting in other peoples' countries."

Manny was tired of arguing. "I know it's bad in Mexico," he said.

"It's bad in Guatemala and Honduras, too," Reina said, "and a couple other countries I could name—and the United States is the market for these drugs. You know, sophisticated Mexicans look at our drug war and see it as an American plan to keep Mexico a third world country."

"Why?" Manny was giving her the cop look now, the look cops give criminals who blame society for their own decision to hotwire a car or hurt their children, or steal, or murder—or do drugs.

"I don't mind the cop look at all," Reina said, looking at Manny with her large green eyes. "I have compassion for all persons bound to the rock of concrete thinking while the complex realities of the real world peck at their liver."

"Uh-huh," Manny said. "Mexico is so much more corrupt than the United States there is no comparison—and I have some tolerance for that because I've lived on the border all my life, but it's still their problem, Reina. It's their job to fix it. What do your sophisticated Mexicans say about that?"

"You're right," Reina said, "but think about how it plays out for us when we have a weak country with great natural resources as a neighbor. It means no labor unions, a dirt cheap labor force, cheaper produce, cheaper oil—all the benefits that come to a little bunch of guys who sit at the top on both sides of the line. We fight a drug war, it keeps them off balance, and they can't build a strong, independent country that competes with ours."

Manny hesitated for a moment, staring down at Reina's bed sheets. "My cousin Carlito sells dope over here for those cartel guys in Sonora. Everybody in our family knows it. Carlito was always a punk. If it was my job to bust him and I could make the case I'd arrest him like anybody else."

Reina looked startled. "Carlito, your cousin who drinks too much at parties? Carlito?" Reina put her hand on Manny's shoulder.

"Yeah," Manny said. "Him. I guess Carlito learned not to talk to you, though." Manny was smiling now.

"Yes he did," Reina said. "I put some attitude on that little bastard. I don't like drunks."

"Want to turn on the National Geographic Channel and watch Border Wars tonight—after you take me where I want to go?" Manny began fondling Reina.

"No, Manny, here's what we're going to do," Reina said, moving in against him. "We're going to go to sleep—unless you've told me again how we stop the drug wars."

"Don't play," Manny said, trying to pull Reina's rear end into his groin. "Nobody is going to stop the Drug wars. We all make too much money—Jeff included. Catch our boss talking with the other lawyers and you will hear them telling each other that drug busts are all they have to make a living."

"Tell me!" Reina pulled back and placed her long, sharp fingernails on Manny's lower abdomen.

"Take the money out of drugs by legalizing and taxing some drugs, decriminalizing other drugs, and making addiction a medical problem," Manny said.

"And what else?"

"Use the money we now spend on law enforcement to rehab drug addicts and to take care of their children—until these addicts can function again, Reina—if they ever can."

"And the rest of it is all about what I'm going to do to you tonight," Reina said. "See how a spoonful full of sugar makes the medicine go down?"

"I only said it because I want you," Manny said.

"Go ahead," Reina said, caressing him. "Save your pride."

Chapter Nine

Devin Woods's speeding ticket had faded a little in the process of being faxed to the offices of the Goldman law firm, but Reina could read it just fine when she picked it off the fax machine the next morning.

"That's the day Lois was killed," Manny said, looking over her shoulder, "and we've got a TO officer named Lopez who wrote that ticket. I'll call Tellez in Ajo and see if I can get permission to be around when they talk to Devin Woods."

***

Tucson to Ajo on AZ-86 was a three-hour run, counting a bathroom break, which Manny made near Gu Vo and subsequently explained to the Border Patrol, who saw him pull over and disappear behind a creosote bush. By the time he got back to his truck, the men in green were parked and waiting for him.

***

"I didn't do nothing," Devin Woods said, when he'd been seated in front of his audience in the Ajo's station's interview room. Devin was looking at three big men, all of them scary. "Who's he?" Devin said, pointing at Manny. Devin already knew Officer Tellez and Lieutenant Davis, the station commander—a little matter of prior contact with law enforcement.

"He's an investigator," Lieutenant Davis said, jerking his chin at Manuel Aguilar. "You saw him before, when we arrested you— but you forgot. Because you do a lot of drugs, Devin." Davis tipped his head toward Manny. "He's wondering about that speeding ticket you got on the TO Nation awhile back. What were you doing over there?"

"Nothing," Devin said.

"That's a brilliant response, Mr. Woods," Lieutenant Davis said.

It went on like that for two hours until Devin confessed.

"What did you do with her ring?" Manny asked the sweating methamphetamine enthusiast.

"What ring?" Devin said. "I never did nothing."

"So you shot a woman through the windshield of her car but you didn't cut off her finger to get her wedding ring, is that right?" Officer Tellez asked.

"No, I didn't do that," Devin said.

"Just to clear it up here, Devin," the lieutenant said, "you say you shot her, but you didn't steal her ring and you didn't set her car on fire, right?"

"I just shot her," Devin said. "Them Indians gave me a ticket and that's what they got back." Devin started laughing.

"My Yaqui grandmother would love you for that," Manny said.

"What's a 'Yaqui'?" Devin asked. He was still laughing.

"My Apache great-grandfather would love you for that, too, Mr. Woods," Tellez said.

"This is not good for you, Devin," Lieutenant Davis said. "You've just told us you committed a hate crime against a Native American and the penalties for hate crimes...well, you just won't ever get out of federal prison. We believe you also committed a heinous crime, as we call it here in Arizona, whether you want to tell us about cutting off Lois Donahue's finger or not. We'll try to help you if you can be truthful with us about the details."

Devin laughed. "I got a finger for you," he said, but he didn't have the courage to make the gesture to emphasize the remark because now Lieutenant Davis was smiling. Lieutenant Davis stared at Devin Woods and smiled until even Devin Woods, through the chemical train wreck of his drug addled brain, could see a murder conviction, a windowless cell on death row, and a lethal injection going into his arm.

"Fade to black, Devin," Tellez said, as if reading what was left of Devin's mind. Lieutenant Davis jerked his chin at the door and Tellez rose and opened it and called down the hall in a soft voice, "Need a Folger Adam here."

A jailer appeared and led Devin away.

After Devin was gone, Lieutenant Davis leaned into Tellez's face and smirked. "You got an Apache great-grandfather?"

Tellez shrugged. "That's what they tell me."

"So this is not a Wounded Knee Scarpini story?"

"Old West history. Back in the day they liked to play. Just like now." Tellez turned to Manny. "There was a Border Patrol agent out here, at the big BP station down the road on 85. You saw it on the way in. Scarpini. He was from the East coast. Kept saying he was part Native American. He was screwing around out at the Virgil Ellis range north of town. Had an AD doing a fast draw. Cut a groove in the side of his knee. We started calling him Wounded Knee Scarpini."

"We thought he was all thumbs when it came to firearms safety," the lieutenant said.

"But not anymore," Tellez said.

"Because two weeks later," the lieutenant said, "Scarpini blew off one thumb shooting two sixguns cowboy style."

Tellez gave Manny a deadpan look. "They reattached it. He can move it a little now." Tellez lifted one large hand and rocked his thumb back and forth.

***

Manny left town after he watched Devin Woods sign a statement, a copy of which might eventually find its way to the offices of the Goldman law firm. Manny had also watched Lieutenant Davis place a call to the FBI, who would not be long in responding to Ajo for a serious talk with Devin Woods.

As pleasant as it might be to contemplate a solved case, Manny doubted Devin Woods was telling the truth. He suspected Woods of using the crazed logic one would need to believe a murder confession would make fools out of law enforcement. Every cop in Arizona knew about the 1991 Buddhist temple massacre outside of Phoenix. Early on, Maricopa County Sheriff's detectives had threatened, coerced, and pressured six young men into false confessions, using marathon-length interrogation sessions in the process. Maricopa County later paid 2.8 million dollars in damages. False confessions came from bad police work—or from nuts. Devin Woods was certainly nuts and he'd confessed after a mere two-hour conversation.

Manny kept heading east, bored with rez radio and desert scenery. He was still miles from Sells when he thought about Evelyn Antone. The little sister. The woman who said Lois Donahue had been the one who took trips to Ajo. Trouble was, people in Ajo recognized Evelyn Antone in the photographs Manny showed them. Not Lois. Beyond that detail, Manny knew it would help the investigation if anyone close to Lois Donahue, the deceased, recognized Devin Woods, the man who had confessed to killing Lois.

Manny reached Sells and the TO police station in late afternoon. He asked for clearance to stop by Evelyn Antone's residence and show her a photograph of Devin Woods. He explained to yellow- eyed Lieutenant Norris that Devin Woods had signed a statement. Norris let Manny stand in the chairless lobby for twenty minutes while he called the FBI and PCSD, Ajo, to verify Manny's claim. Manny spent the time talking to the receptionist, a voluptuous woman who smiled and laughed and occasionally tossed her rich black hair. Manny was considering asking her why Norris was so chronically pissed off when Norris himself came back through a door of the type favored by law enforcement—heavy metal, thick, tiny or no window, your choice of gray or beige.

"Let me see those photos of your guy," the lieutenant said, giving Manny a look as flat and cold as the door he'd just come through.

Manny showed Norris the photos. "You got an extra copy?" Norris asked.

Manny handed Norris an extra copy. "I'll show it to the patrol officers and the Criminal Investigators," Norris said. "Go see Evelyn Antone." Norris went back through the heavy door, the photo in his hand.

"Thanks," Manny said to Norris's back. Manny meant it. He'd just witnessed one glimmer of cooperation from TO police in the matter of clearing Donald Donahue.

***

Manny noticed Evelyn Antone's door was ajar before he got out of his truck. Not a good sign, but maybe not a bad one. He stepped out of the truck on the side away from the house and called Evelyn's name. There was no response. Manny considered rummaging under his seat for the lockbox containing his handguns and decided against it.

"Evelyn," Manny called. Now he was at her door. Beige, hollow core, old paint and life's usual scuff marks. He knocked. When there was no response, he stepped inside and saw Evelyn Antone lying in the middle of her living room. She'd fallen among her nephew's toys. The blood spread across her face had dried and what looked like a bullet entry wound in her face was dry as well. Apparently, someone had shot Evelyn Antone many hours before. Manny evaluated all this at the speed of light, deciding not to assume the killer was still in the house and make a run for the door, his truck, and his weapon.

He circled around the body on tiptoe, watching where he put his boots. Then he squatted, facing the entrance of Evelyn Antone's little house. A black Glock pistol lay beside Evelyn with its trigger forward and sliver of brass and copper visible in the space between the lower and upper part of the gun. Manny knew he was looking at a self-loading pistol, almost certainly the one used to kill Evelyn, and that the weapon had a live round in its barrel, waiting for someone to pull the trigger.

Gangland style, Manny was thinking. Shoot somebody with a throw-away gun, a gun that can't be traced to the shooter unless the cops find it in the shooter's possession, throw the gun down, and leave—all the choices you could make in your life, Manny thought, and you make the choice to murder. Then he remembered Jonas. Reina would be shocked and angry with him for forgetting a child while analyzing a crime scene.

"Jonas," Manny called softly. He turned his head toward the bedrooms and called again. He heard a revolver being cocked, the sound coming from the doorway, and he lunged sideways and grabbed the Glock as his hearing disappeared in the wake of gunfire in the small room. Manny hit the floor sideways and shot at the big shadow in the door, the man with the gun, and the man staggered backwards and fell outside, out of sight.

Manny got his legs under him and jumped up, keeping the Glock pointed at the door. Daylight fell on the dirt yard and Donald Donahue lay there under the sullen winter sun. The revolver lay a foot away from his right hand.

"I didn't shoot her," Manny said, kicking the revolver farther away as he kneeled beside Donny.

Donny mumbled and his head lolled but he was looking in Manny's face. "She was dead when I got here," Manny went on. "The blood on her face was dry, Donny. I'm calling it in, you hold on. Hold on."

Manny called 911 and stuck his fingers in Donald Donahue's wounds and talked to him until Lieutenant Norris and two big TOPD cops arrived. Manny knew TOPD would be coming in with their holsters unsnapped and he opened his hands as much as he could with his fingers still stuck in Donny's wounds. The TO cops could see he had no gun and wasn't about to reach for one. Manny kept his fingers stuck in Donny's wounds, both of them chest wounds, neither of them near the heart.

"Just stay like you are," Lieutenant Norris said to Manny. He turned to the younger TOPD officer. "Watch him, "Norris said, and jerked his head at Manny. "Take the back," Norris said to the other officer. Norris waited until the officer drew a weapon and disappeared behind Evelyn Antone's little house. Then Norris gave Manny a profoundly dirty look and went through the front door of

Evelyn Antone's little house with his gun in his hand. Norris was still inside when the ambulance rolled up a couple of minutes later.

"Don't go to sleep, Donny," Manny was saying again and again when the EMT's knelt beside them. "Stay awake."

The EMT's worked at getting Donny on a stretcher and one of them, at Norris's request, took swabs of Manny's bloody fingers, then wetted a sterile cloth and handed it to him. "Anything hurt anywhere?" the EMT asked. "Any cuts on your hands?" Manny shook his head. He kept wiping with the cloth even after the blood was gone. When he felt a touch on his arm and saw the EMT holding out a plastic bag, Manuel Aguilar realized he was in shock and he'd have to concentrate like a technical diver working at 300 feet. "Put it in here," the EMT said. Then the ambulance was gone and Manny was again face to face with Lieutenant Norris.

"You're familiar with term 'investigative detention,' Aguilar," Norris said. "Turn around, put your hands behind your back, palms out." Norris cuffed Manny and Mirandized him. "You're not under arrest, Aguilar," Norris said. "Not yet, anyway, so don't worry about jail right now, worry about being in an incriminating situation. Do I have your permission to search you, your cell phone and your vehicle?"

"Yes," Manny said.

Norris led Manny to a cage car and frisked him. The two large TOPD officers who had responded with Norris stood by and watched, functioning as both witnesses and cover men. Manny knew they'd beat the crap out of him or shoot him if he made one wrong move. They would also bury him in court if he said anything incriminating or had any incriminating evidence on his person. Norris took his cell phone and his keys.

"I'll be back," Norris said. He put Manny in the cage car and slammed the door extra hard. Manny thought Norris was gone until he was startled by a tap on the car window and turned his head to find Norris banging on it with Manny's own cell phone. Norris bent down and brought the pupils of his scary yellow eyes level with the pupils of Manny's eyes. "One more thing, Aguilar," Norris said. "Every time I turn around it's *you*." Then he strode off.

Norris was back in one minute. "What's in the lock box under your car seat?" Manny told him and Norris shouted, "Open it!" at a TOPD uniform who was standing by Manny's truck.

More officers arrived, including the FBI Evidence Response Team, most of them dressed in blue jackets with yellow letters reading *FBI* writ large in several places on the jackets. All but two of the ERT people started processing the scene. The two who didn't, a tall white man wearing generic civilian clothing and a gun under his blue FBI jacket, and a short white woman, also dressed in civvies and gun, her FBI ball cap pulled low over her pitiless lavender eyes, stood by the patrol car while a TOPD officer got Manny out of it. Then the perennially pissed off Lieutenant Norris appeared. Time for The Talk.

 Manny went over it and over it, explaining why he showed up at Evelyn Antone's house and going on to recount the sequence of events as he best remembered them. The Talk took two hours. The sun was home drinking peppermint tea when they finally stopped and the Evidence Response Team was using high intensity lights. Had Manny made any inconsistent statements the interview would have taken longer and then he would have gone to jail. Everybody fell silent when they finally wheeled Evelyn Antone's body out on a gurney. After that, the FBI and the TOPD confirmed they had Manny's contact information and told him he could go, making it clear they'd be in touch—real soon.

Manny took back his keys and his cell phone, knowing the TOPD had done a quick manual check of its history. He also knew the FBI team had initiated mobile device forensics on his cell phone. A bit-for-bit copy of its contents now lived in an FBI laptop—along with a copy of everything on his laptop as well. He went to his truck. They'd taken his guns for evidence so he closed his empty lock box and began putting the tossed truck back together. Then he called Reina with the bad news.

"Reina."

"What's wrong?"

"How do you know something's wrong?"

"Your voice, honey," Reina said, almost wearily. "Your voice."

"I only said one word," Manny muttered. He realized he was dazed, exhausted.

"I love you, Manny," Reina said. She was talking slowly now and pronouncing her words distinctly. "Tell me."

Manny took a breath and started talking. "Devin Woods confessed to murdering Lois Donahue. I stopped by Evelyn Antone's house to show her Devin's mugshot. Jonas, the kid, was not at Evelyn's, Reina. He's not in this. He's with other relatives. Evelyn's front door was open. I knocked, I called her name, I stepped inside. I found Antone dead, shot to death. Donald Donahue came through Antone's front door and shot at me. I shot back. I think he just lost it and reacted. I didn't recognize him. He was backlit, front of his body in shadow. I reacted, I shot back. He's wounded. He's in the hospital. I just finished with the TOPD and the FBI. Do you know why Donahue was out of jail?"

"Well, are you sure you're not hurt or in shock? You can drive home okay?" Reina said.

"Yeah, I'm fine. How did Donahue get out?"

"Jeff and I haven't heard anything. I'll call him tonight and let him know what happened. We'll call the US Attorney's office tomorrow, Manny. Get home safe." Reina pressed the end button and speed dialed Jeff Goldman's personal phone.

"He shot the frigging *client*?" Goldman said. "We should have told him not to shoot anybody," he added, after he'd heard the story. "See you both tomorrow. Nineish? We'll go over it and find out how Donald Donahue got out of jail."

"Yeah," Reina said. "Sorry, Jeff."

***

"How are you doing?" Reina asked Manny, after he had curled up on the couch with Reina—a couch flanked by Goldie the Golden Retriever and Grayboy, the cat, who, like Reina, gave Manny an inquiring stare.

"I could make a light bulb dim right now," Manny said glumly.

"Makes perfect sense," Reina said, looking around, "but they don't look any dimmer to me."

"That's because they're already dim and you can see in the dark," Manny said.

"Why don't we go to bed?" Reina said. Goldie the dog and Grayboy the cat both looked toward the bedroom, then back at Manny and Reina.

Manny's cell phone rang as he was getting to his feet. Manny turned the phone in his hand so Reina could see the display screen. Manny's father calling. Manny sat down on the couch and took the call. Reina and the animals began drifting toward the bedroom.

"Somebody's got to go to Nogales and pick up Carlito," Manny's father said.

"Why?" Manny snapped.

"Because he's your cousin, Manuel, that's why. It's Carlito," Manny's father said, and began talking in Spanish. "He was into something—"

"Carlito's been into something all his life," Manny said, speaking in English.

"Just hold on, Manny," Jesus Aguilar said, "be patient. Think about Alma and Luis. Carlito was cheating some guys in Sonora. They came up here and got him. They tricked him. They told him to come across the line and go to a party. They been holding him for three days. We got his house and his cars signed over to them. Your brother Reggie put up some money. Alma and Luis had to give them money, too. Alma is my sister and she is your aunt. Think about her. Think about your Uncle Luis. "

"Carlito gets everybody in trouble and everybody has to pay—especially Alma and Luis," Manny said. "Why didn't I hear about this before and what do you want me to do?"

"We didn't want to tell everybody right away, Manny. We were busy trying to take care of it. Carlito just called. They let him go. He's in Nogales on this side of the line. He's only got his clothes and his driver's license. He needs somebody to go pick him up. Alma and Luis are old, I'm home with your mom, you know, and your brother Reggie's got a family. Can you go down there?"

"Where is he?" Manny said.

"He told Alma he's at a Denny's on Grand Avenue."

"Okay, Dad. We won't be back until pretty late. I'll call you when I've got him."

"Call Alma," Jesus said.

"If I call Alma," Manny said, "she'll be processing this whole thing with Carlito on my phone all the way back to Tucson. I don't want to hear it."

Manuel Aguilar's father was a Korean War vet who went to work in the San Manuel Copper Mine when he came home to Arizona. He spent thirty years as a miner, living in Tucson to be with his family, carpooling back and forth for the one and one quarter hour drive north to San Manuel. "What do you mean 'processing'?" he said.

"Talking about her feelings," Manny said. "People talk about a traumatic incident until they feel better— or worse, or whatever. It's good for people, but I'll have to listen to Carlito all the way back the way it is now. Work with me on this, Dad. Let me just call you and leave it there. Now, since Carlito's little horse farm got signed over to the cartel, where do I drop him off?"

"Drop him at Alma and Luis's," Manny's father said. "They'll be waiting up."

Manny snapped his cell phone shut and went in the bedroom, muttering about dumbasses. Reina was looking real good, Manny thought, just as she was, sitting on the bed in a cozy, nondescript nightgown. The cat and the dog were already in place—the dog in a corner, the cat on the bed.

Reina looked at him. "Going to Nogales?"

Manny started laughing. "Well, it's better than crying," he said, when he had stopped. "Carlito is a *pendejo*. Carlito—" Manny held up his hand with his thumb and finger held two inches apart, as if he were measuring something, "is that one last stupid hair that just hangs down—"

"I guess I won't ask from where," Reina said.

"No," Manny said. "Don't ask. Carlito can't be happy making money pushing cartel dope. He has to skim. He has to steal from them. They took all his property and let him go. I have to pick him up. Don't wait up for me."

"He's in Arizona?" Reina asked.

"Yeah, he got back on the American side with only his driver's license and his usual load of bullshit," Manny said. He turned to leave, reaching for his jacket. "I'll see you later tonight." Then he turned back and bent over and kissed her. "Thanks, Reina," he said.

She watched him leave.

Chapter Ten

"What took you so long," Carlito said, when Manny found him leaning on a table at Denny's, talking to a couple of other night owls he'd drawn into his circle of charm—even though, Manny reflected, Carlito didn't have any money.

"You ready to go?" Manny said.

Carlito stood about five foot seven. He had dark hair and happy eyes—although one of his eyes was black and his face was bruised. The eyes of a bullshitter, Manny thought, looking at him. Carlito was a family legend. It was said by Carlito's father and his uncles and male cousins that Carlito could pack ten pounds of shit into a five pound bag. Carlito was always talking—and looking for criminal schemes, drunk and horny women, or a line of blow. All three at once? A trifecta for Carlito, Manny thought, sourly. And *Fumar marijuana* was a given, Manny added, closing out his own interior monologue, smoking marijuana was every day for *mi querido primo* Carlito.

"Could you loan me a couple bucks for the coffees?" Carlito said. "These guys bought a round and I owe them one."

By way of reply, Manny stepped over to the waitress and pointed at Carlito, "How much do I owe you for that guy's tab?"

The waitress pulled the bill out of her apron. "Fourteen seventy-eight," she said tonelessly, staring at Carlito like he was a pile of rotting fish heads.

"Hey," Carlito said, grinning, "I was hungry. I had the waffles, okay? And the bacon. What the hell, man. See, I told you," he went on, addressing the waitress now, "that I can wash the dishes if my cousin here don't show up. But he showed up, so it's all good." Carlito turned to the two idiots at his table. "Right, guys?" The two idiots nodded dully, their eyes on Manny, who was obviously some kind of cop, and a big, bad pissed off looking cop at that.

Manny gave the waitress a twenty. Then he gave Carlito the evil eye until the punk shook hands with the idiots and headed for the door. Manny walked behind him, shocked, depressed and exhausted from shooting his employer's client, spending hours at the crime scene, then driving from Ajo, while saying foxhole religion prayers for Donald Donahue all the way back to Tucson. Then, driving to Nogales—another hour and ten minutes on the road.

"Man, it was a long walk up here to Denny's," Carlito said, limping slightly as he made for Manny's truck in the lonesome yellow light of the parking lot, "but I really wanted some of them waffles."

Manny wanted to wait until Carlito reached the truck and then slam him against the side of it and tell him what a little prick he was.

"Fasten your seatbelt," Manny said, when Carlito had drug himself into the truck seat. Carlito complied, hair falling over his forehead, half his face in darkness.

"Man, I'm glad you picked me up," Carlito said. "They had me blindfolded the whole time. I could hear the radio in the other room playing, like, *Brown Eyed Girl*. I'm listening to that and it was all I had to keep me going."

"What's your plan, Carlito?" Manny said, turning his key in the ignition of his old Ford.

"What plan?" Carlito said, responding the same way he'd responded back in grade school when the bus driver had asked him the same question. That time, Carlito had been carving up the seats with a pocketknife. Manny, then a child riding on the same bus, remembered the incident. Carlito, of course, did not.

"Your plan to pay back your parents and half of your other relatives," Manny said. "Your plan to make up for what you did to their lives?"

Carlito started talking. Manny ignored him, drew his cell phone, used it with one hand, and drove with the other. It was a short conversation with Manny's father, as promised. Manny had Carlito. He would drop Carlito at his parents' house. By the time

Manny and Carlito were pulling into Tucson they were sharing a few jokes. Carlito would be Carlito. Manny would be Manny. Family would be family. Manny walked Carlito into Alma and Luis's house, said some kind words to them, and left the perennially defective Carlito in the arms of his grateful and aging parents.

***

Just after midnight Manny parked and locked his truck, opened Reina's gate, and came quietly into her house, a place of night lights and dark red kilims spread on dark red tile floors. Goldie's nails made a clicking sound as she came from the bedroom to greet Manny. The cat followed. Manny slipped off his clothes and got into bed and Reina, half-awake, held him and looked into his eyes.

"As Carlito would say," Manny said, "it's all good."

"Mmm," Reina said and pretended to sleep, keeping herself attuned to Manny's mood, aura, and whatever else a more than human woman like herself could keep track of, all at the same time.

Manny turned over and pretended to sleep. The image of a wounded and bloody Donald Donahue appeared and disappeared in Manny's mind. Like there's a light switch, Manny thought, and somebody is turning it on and off. He kept hearing words he had heard said, years before, when a fellow sheriff's officer had been wounded while doing a traffic stop: *He could never do much after he was shot.* Law enforcement can get a medical retirement, a paycheck, if gunshot wounds make them unfit for further duty. Manny knew that Donald Donahue, a cowboy, could not. At least, Manny thought, Donahue has his tribe, if he can't go back to work.

After a while, pretending to sleep got the best of Manny and he did sleep, lulled by the sound of Grayboy purring at the foot of the bed.

Later, in dreamtime, in dream space, he relived the day's

horrors and came at last to a vision of a dark figure, a vague silhouette against a twilight sky over what seemed like Ajo, Arizona. The figure held something but Manny couldn't see what it was.

***

Manny was awake and drinking coffee in Reina's kitchen the next morning when he remembered the last part of the dream. Oh well, he thought, no choice but to wait for the next dream. He knew from experience that one would be coming—and that, like most of his dreams, it wouldn't be fun.

Manny was bent over, feeding Grayboy the cat a can of exorbitantly high priced salmon, when his cell phone vibrated on Reina's kitchen counter. Manny grabbed it and flipped it open.

"This is a heads up for you," Officer Tellez said. "Devin Woods recanted his confession. We started checking with TOPD and the timelines weren't matching up. We can't put Devin anywhere but on the highway, driving. Neither can TOPD. He got his speeding ticket after the report of the car fire, but he'd been speeding an hour before—when he blew by a TOPD officer who called ahead to another officer. The second officer actually wrote the speeding ticket and the elapsed time between observation and actual contact is consistent with travel on State Route 86 at a steady seventy miles an hour."

Manny thanked Tellez and hung up. That about does it, he thought. It can always get worse, but this is close enough.

"Who was that? Reina called from the bathroom.

"It was Tellez, PCSD, Ajo. Devin Woods didn't kill Lois. PCSD ran the timelines against his contacts with TOPD on the rez. He was on the highway. Woods is crazy, but he sounded truthful when he made his confession."

"Under British law they don't even enter confessions into evidence," Reina said, in a tone that was a trifle too off hand for Manny's mood at that moment.

"Yeah?" Manny said. "Do they still hang people over there?

Because if they do, I'd like to ship them Devin Woods and a few other criminals." He could feel Reina doing an eye roll in the bathroom mirror.

* * *

Jeff Goldman was already in his office when Manny and Reina came in at nine. It was cold and everybody was grim. Goldman stood in the door of his office wearing a white shirt with no tie and a dark blue vest. For as lean as he was, Goldman seemed not bothered by the cold, Reina thought, watching him.

"Come in," Goldman said. Manny and Reina took seats and Goldman moved behind his desk, sat in his chair, and put his feet up on the desk. "The prosecution cut Donny Donahue loose after they took statements from a couple of Border Patrol spotters," Goldman began. He laid his hands in his lap, interlocked his fingers, and began tapping his thumbs together. "Initially, these spotters had called in the car fire that burned up Lois. They had no eyes on it, but they were the first to see the smoke. TOPD went over it with the BP but the Border Patrol didn't mention they'd noticed Donny riding in the area for the entire hour previous. Eventually, when the FBI went over it again with the Border Patrol, this lone cowboy thing came up and the feds and the TO Criminal Investigators realized the BP spotters had eyes on Donny the whole time. They conferenced with the US Attorney's office and TOPD let Donny out of the jailhouse in Sells—prematurely, for our purposes—and without notifying us, of course." Goldman stared past Manny and Reina, looking out the door of his office at nothing in particular. Then he looked at Manny. "Have you called the hospital about Donahue's condition?" Manny shook his head. "Good," Goldman said. "You can bet they don't want to hear from the shooter. Reina?" Reina shook her head. Goldman took his feet off his desk and made the call. Donald Donahue was hanging on, albeit with his lungs punctured and his ribs broken by two 9 millimeter bullets.

"I got a call from PCSD in Ajo this morning," Manny said.

"Devin Woods made a false confession. PCSD double checked with the Tohono O'odham PD. Devin was on the highway when Lois's car went up in flames."

"Be that as it may, our role," Goldman said, bending forward and placing resting his forearms on his desk, "in the defense of Donald Donahue is over. He's no longer a suspect in his wife's murder. Now, assuming Manny will be cleared of blame in this tragic incident which left our former client badly wounded—" Goldman paused for effect, "where does that leave us?" Goldman looked from one to the other, from Reina to Manny, before staring out his open door, into the front office of the Goldman Law Firm, past Reina's work station, and out the window at the blue winter sky of Tucson. Soft light fell on his serene white face.

Jeff Goldman, Reina thought, watching him with her green eyes, a man fed up with the reactionary, mean, petty, and corrupt Arizona political establishment, a man drawn to underdogs, a man who loved doing a litigational boot party, when he could, on the heads of whining prosecutors and perverted judges. A man who could dream, as Manny and Reina did, of a clear blue sky, sweet as mother's milk, know it would never happen, and fly in it anyway—ride some thermals above the nastiness—and Jeff could do all this and sleep with an attractive female prosecutor—and the prosecutor could be happy sleeping with Jeff. No matter where you go, Reina thought, there you are.

Manuel Aguilar, meanwhile, was taking in what Goldman meant. Goldman was giving his investigator, Manuel Aguilar, a chance to work off a moral debt—a debt incurred accidentally, perhaps, but still....

"It leaves us with who killed Lois Donahue and Evelyn Antone," Manny said.

"I would like you to work on solving those murders," Goldman said. "Do it when not working on other cases as I may assign them. I will volunteer to pay your expenses if you volunteer to work on this extraneous matter without pay. If you have to be out in the middle of nowhere—Ajo, for example, Reina can trundle down to the court house if she can't get what we need out of the computer. If I need you to do electronic surveillance, you'll have to come back and do it. I can't have Reina sitting in cars in the middle of the night with binoculars and listening devices. Right, Reina?"

"Not unless I'm watching cute guys with hard flat stomachs slip boxer shorts off their narrow hips to expose their vibrant manhood," Reina said.

"Does that sound fair to you?" Goldman said, looking at Manny.

Manny nodded.

"Good. Now, Reina. First, please remain appropriate with your verbalizations. Second, call Johnny Oaks, hire him to attend Lois Donahue's funeral so he can watch who shows up— disaffected relatives, former lovers, the murderer, that sort of thing.

"Now, let's go to work on what we do here every day," Goldman said. "Ninety to ninety-five percent of Federal drug smuggling cases—that's *Federal* cases, the expensive ones for the taxpayers—here in Tucson are for marijuana smuggling. There's some meth, but mostly marijuana.

"So, it should be no surprise to you that I have a brief to prepare regarding a young man who will probably do a five year bounce for smuggling marijuana from Mexico. Yes, that's five years for smuggling marijuana, a plant with both psychoactive and healing qualities which has been prohibited in this country since the 1937—" Goldman interlaced his fingers and snapped his knuckles, "and which everybody has used, at one time or another, including lots of cops. But, as we attorneys like to say, during lunch and off the record—what else have we got to pay the bills?

"Pursuant to the case I have after the meth freak, Manny, I need you to do a court records search on still another mule, albeit a blind mule this time, in yet another smuggling bust, who tells me that, being a guy out of work, he answered an ad in a Tucson paper, seeking a driver for a two and a half ton truck that needed to go over to Los Angeles. He was then caught in that Border

Patrol flytrap on Interstate 8. Because he was headed toward California, he wasn't initially stopped. Trouble was, the truck smelled so much like pot that a sniff dog alerted on it from two traffic lanes away. I believe the guy's innocent. He wouldn't be the first naïve and out of work person who tried a make a few bucks driving a truck somewhere for someone he didn't know. I'm considering getting an allergy doc to testify as to this guy's ability to smell."

Reina nodded. "Now, would that be the Border Patrol flytrap where they dump felony charges on incoming Californians found to be in possession of legal cannabis and confiscate their California state issued medical marijuana cards as well?"

"The very one," Goldman said.

Manny stared at nothing and waited for his lover and his boss to get done doing cannabis comedy. Finally, Goldman handed Manny a sheet of paper. Manny and Reina wheeled out of Goldman's office, pausing to touch noses and lips by Reina's desk. Then, Manny was out the door, heading downtown for Tucson's pink-domed courthouse.

***

It was three days before he had a chance to get out to Ajo and the night before he left, he talked it over with Reina while they nested in her sunken living room, amongst the cat, the dog, and a little bit of candlelight.

"Goldman can spare you, I'd rather not," Reina said, "but if you have to go, then you do. You've told me Evelyn Antone was in this mess, somehow but definitely. What about that?"

Manny was watching Grayboy the cat who was watching the bubbles in Manny's beer glass. "Beck, the drug counselor your friend George knows, recognized Evelyn. So did Tellez, PSCD, Ajo. She's the one who'd been going out to Ajo, not Lois. Nobody in Ajo recognized Lois Donahue—not a single soul. Evelyn withheld information."

Chapter Eleven

Bud Beck's old aluminum trailer look deserted when Manny stopped his truck in front of it. Manny got out and knocked, then banged, on the thin door. Still no response. Manny looked over his shoulder and saw the fedora man. The fedora man was sitting in his trailer, gesturing for Manny to come over.

"You're that fella' Manny, right? Beck went back to Washington state," the fedora man said, when Manny had walked over, opened the trailer door, and stood there, watching the fedora man. The man was composed, relaxed, but his voice sounded like he didn't use it much. Almost a hermit, Manny thought, sitting in a trailer all day. "He left this for you." The fedora man pointed at his table, a table that looked much like Beck's had looked—a clutter of gadgets, tools, old paperbacks, the usual coffee pot. The fedora man was pointing at the smaller of two fixed blade hunting knives. Manny recognized the scaled down knife that Beck had worn.

"Why'd he go to Washington?" Manny asked.

"Had family business," the man said. "Said he didn't know when he'd be back."

"What's your name?" Manny asked.

"Stovall," the man said. "I come down here every winter to get out of the cold."

"Does Bud have a forwarding address?"

"Not that I know of," Stovall said. "They might have somethin' up at the office."

"Did Bud tell you why he left this for me?"

"Nope," Stovall said, and his old man's eyes came up from under his hat and grazed Manny's face. "If you don't want it I'll hold onto it." Stovall was smiling now.

Manny took the knife and left. When he'd gotten into his truck he sat and turned the sheathed knife over in his hands. He drew the knife and looked up and down the blade and at the handle. He got a compact flashlight out and shined it into the sheath. There was nothing. He sheathed the knife and snapped the restraining strap and turned the sheathed knife over in his hands again. He pushed on the top of the belt loop until it bowed out and looked at the inside surface of the loop. The printing was faint and small and appeared as if it had been done with a common ballpoint pen: *Walker.*

Casually mindful that the name inside the belt loop belonged to a lot of people, most notably William Walker, Ajo's reporter at large for The Copper News, Manny did what detectives do. He assumed nothing about the writing on the belt loop—or about anything else that came under his purview. In addition, he never believed anyone, ever, outside of his girlfriend, his boss, and his parents. No law enforcement person would have been surprised when Manny jumped on the last person in the knife's chain of custody—Stovall.

"Come on in—again," Stovall said when Manny knocked. Stovall was smiling when Manny's bulk nearly filled the trailer on Stovall's side of the door.

"Mr. Stovall, do you know why someone would write a name in ballpoint pen on the inside of this belt loop?" Manny held up the sheathed knife and pointed at the belt loop.

"Nope," Stovall said, appearing not to take offense or show any alarm, "but it sure seems like you're in a lather about somebody giving you a knife. I'd quit worryin' if I were you—makes ya' old."

Manny left, having seen nothing with his cop's third eye that implicated Stovall in anything. He checked at the office of the Coyote Howls. He asked nothing about Stovall but requested contact information about Beck, saying he was a friend who had come calling. For his trouble, Manny got a phone number that didn't work and a post office box in someplace called Concrete, Washington.

He sat in his truck outside the Coyote Howls and called Reina. "Does Jeff need me for anything?"

"Nope," Reina said. "What's up?"

"Take another look at Beck," Manny said. "His cell number doesn't work and he left town. I can find him from here, but see if there's any background on him we didn't catch the first time. And please look at William Walker again."

"You know," Reina said, "CIA guys are forever using being a news reporter as a cover. Maybe Walker is Ajo's resident spook, although I'm sure they don't need one there. What is it about Walker?"

Manny hesitated. He knew how stupid the name on the knife sheath would sound. "Beck left a knife for me. He was wearing it when we talked. Somebody wrote *Walker* inside the belt loop."

"Oh," Reina said, "a c-l-e-w."

"What do you mean?"

"That's how they used to spell *clue*, Manny. It's so Sherlock Holmes—a mysterious scrawl on a special knife. Did you look at it under a magnifying glass?"

"I know, Reina. It sounds crazy. Run the names."

"Come on back to Tucson, Sherlock. I'll give you a funny hat and get you laid."

"You bought yourself a spanking. Get me that information."

"You know what Freud said. Sometimes a cigar is just a cigar."

"What?"

"It's probably just a knife, Manny."

"Run the names." Manny snapped off his cell phone.

"Mm-mmm, wait 'til your daddy gets home," Reina said, to no one in particular, when she had hung up her desk phone.

"Then what happens?" Goldman called out from the back room.

"He's promised me a spanking," Reina said.

"Legal office," Goldman said. "Be appropriate." Goldman put his feet up on his desk and kept on reading a file, happy that his employees were in good enough spirits to make jokes. Goldman knew that Donald Donahue, an innocent—and the guy the Goldman Law Firm had been trying to protect—might never feel like joking again.

Time passed and Reina looked up to see Jeff's 4 o'clock appointment rolling in the door—Marvin Pennywhistle, a man of medium build, his habitual burned-going-to-brown skin contrasting mightily with his dirty, but still white, T shirt. A camouflage baseball cap, jeans, a worn belt, and tan work boots made up the rest of his clothing. Mr. Pennywhistle, Reina noted, glancing at his file, was a craftsman whose occupation was pouring cement. A criminal complaint had been lodged against him for domestic violence.

"Mr. Pennywhistle?"

"Yes," Pennywhistle said. He did not, to his credit, Reina thought, leer at her. He seemed nervous, glancing into all the corners of the room.

"Have a seat if you like. I'll let Mr. Goldman know you're here." Pennywhistle stood and Reina knocked on Jeff's door and leaned around it, half out of Pennywhistle's line of sight. She said something Pennywhistle didn't hear to someone who was completely on the other side of the door. Jeff Goldman emerged from his office, tall, lean, wearing a white shirt with a navy blue tie pulled halfway down his chest. Jeff shook Marvin's hand and ushered him into his office.

After he had closed the door, glancing out as he did so to make sure Reina was well out of earshot, Goldman went around his desk, sat down, leaned across it, and said quietly to Pennywhistle, "You can get a DV for dropping a plate."

"If I get convicted on this one, they'll take my guns."

"We'll see what we can do," Goldman said. "Tell me what happened."

About an hour later, Reina looked up to see Goldman ushering Pennywhistle out. "Yeah, it's true," Goldman was saying. "The BATFE has a system called eTrace. It's internet based and it gives the names and addresses of American first-time firearms purchasers to law enforcement in other countries, including Mexico and Columbia. Even Japan. There's a bilingual version in English and Spanish."

"What the hell?" Pennywhistle said.

"They do it because they believe they can bust gun runners that way," Goldman said. "And the rest of us are supposed to be happy with our names and addresses in the hands of a bunch of corrupt Mexican cops who work for the drug cartels. The cartels get amour piercing weapons so they can shoot through bullet proof vests. They get thousands of AK's and AR's, most of them from sources in the United States. And the BATFE can't stop it. They get in trouble with the Office of the Inspector General for lack of coordination and efficiency. The thing is, Marvin, if the drug wars went away, the gun smuggling problem would largely go away."

"Well," Marvin said, "you can't have people using drugs, Mr. Goldman. My mother-in-law runs a motel. Kids get to smoking marijuana while they're folding towels—right there folding towels and smoking it."

"Take care, Marvin," Goldman said. "We'll be in touch with you next week." Goldman turned back toward his office and let Reina show Pennywhistle the rest of the way out. She remained at the door after she'd closed it, peering out the small window.

"What?" Goldman said.

"I like his bumper sticker," Reina said. *"Don't Believe the Liberal Media.* And he's just standing by his truck, staring all around at the sky."

"He's looking for black helicopters," Goldman muttered, slipping back into his office. "And he has a wife who doesn't like him—maybe he's looking down the street to see if she's trying to run him over."

"I didn't know the BATFE sent your name all over the globe if you buy a gun from a dealer," Reina said.

"There's no privacy left, Reina," Goldman snapped, coming back into the room.

"I know. I've just never heard you mention guns. I know you're not a fan of guns," Reina said.

"Did your father own a gun?"

"Yeah," Reina said. "So?"

"My father owns one," Goldman said. "My grandfather was

the mayor of Nogales. I've got a picture of my grandfather with a bunch of dead ducks, a shotgun, and a shell vest. I don't think, necessarily, that the BATFE is after my grandfather's shotgun, even if he were alive to tell them to get lost when they came for it, but any American's name in the hands of a foreign government, just because of a legal gun purchase, is a gross violation of privacy for me. I'm from the West. We have a lot of responsible gun owners here." Goldman disappeared into his office.

"What about guns that shoot lots of bullets, Jeff? The guns mentally ill people use to kill everybody in sight?" Reina called after him. "I'm really not trying to argue here. I just honestly need to know your answer to that."

Jeff came out of his office a second time. "I'd be for banning those kinds of guns if it would work," he said. "And, sure, let's get serious about background checks. But I think the bottom line is the politicians just asked themselves, 'What's cheaper? Fix the mental health system in this country or talk about firearms legislation?'"

Reina sat down at her keyboard, eyebrows still raised in surprise. Jeff Goldman, a man of parts. She went back to what she'd been working on—William Walker, currently residing in Ajo, Arizona.

***

Manny Aguilar had only one investigative chore, now that he was finished grilling an amused Mr. Stovall about the case of the mysterious miniature hunting knife. He took a gallon-size plastic bag out of his briefcase, put the knife in it, and sealed the bag. He opened his suitcase and gently put the knife in a small, zippered compartment and thought, for a morose moment, about what his life had come to.

He rolled out of the Coyote Howls at five miles an hour. Nobody was really on top of anybody else at the Howls, Manny noted. Acres of flat, nearly barren ground, striated with dirt roads that ran up and down, sometimes practically disappearing in the distance, so roomy was the Coyote Howls. Manny turned onto 85, drove to the Ajo Library, fired up his laptop and jumped on their internet. Time to find Bud Beck.

The Concrete, Washington phone book named no Becks. The Skagit County Assessor's Office yielded no Becks who owned property in Concrete. Manny stepped out through the library door and called a friend in the Postal Inspectors office. Then he went back into the library and waited for his cell phone to vibrate. When it did, a half-hour later, he stepped outside again, listened to his friend, and took down a woman's name—a resident of Concrete, Washington.

＊＊＊

"Bud passed away," the woman said. "We're sending someone down to pick up his things and sell his trailer. He'd been ill for some time. He didn't tell you?"

"He never told me he was ill," Manny said. "My condolences. He left a small hunting knife for me with a neighbor, Mr. Stovall. Did Bud ever mention me? Manny Aguilar?"

"No."

Manny asked for the woman's relationship to Bud—a sister, Ilene. She gave Manny the date of Bud's death and verified that the funeral service was held in Concrete. The obituaries in the Concrete Herald (*The Voice of the Upper Skagit Valley, Born 1901, Reborn 2009*) told him the rest.

Whatever it was about Walker and the magic knife, Manny would have to find out on his own. He reflected that he was here, in Ajo, a sleepy dot on hundreds of square miles of mostly uninhabited desert. He would not have been surprised to see an item in the Copper News noting the discovery of a pair of sandals marked "Property of Jesus Christ. If Found, Please Return." He decided to take a drive north of town and jump off Arizona State Route 85 on a dirt road that ran to a place the map was calling Charley Bell Pass.

An hour later Manny was on higher ground and out of his

truck, walking. Out of habit, he carried a cheap day pack with water. He had dug into his briefcase for the folder with pictures of Lois Donahue and Evelyn Antone. And, out of another habit when walking in the borderlands, he dug out his .45 automatic and slipped it into his belt.

Winter grasses sprouted out of tan desert crust. Sunlight softened by high, thin clouds threw gentle shadows on the east side of giant saguaros, shadows that pointed toward a vast desert basin in which parts of the town of Ajo could be seen as a clutter of tiny cream colored boxes, with the low desert continuing for miles on the other side of those boxes and finally curling up into a purplish wave of ridge line, beyond which a watcher could only imagine more basin, and then, at last, the points of mountains against the sky.

Manny was curious when he saw the small white building— almost too small for an ordinary ranch house, he thought. The place looked more like a big old bunkhouse, probably built of abode brick, but definitely sealed over with a flat, grayish-white plaster that seemed to somehow absorb light, rather than reflect it. The roof was tin and a large chimney was stuck on the outside of the north wall.

The little rancho looked deserted and no flag hung from a flag pole, painted a flat white, and standing at the edge of the porch. Manny could see no road or trail going in or out. No vehicle was visible but the ruin of a Chevrolet truck, rusted into sculpture.   A spectral relic, made in the days when liquor was illegal. The days when bootleggers got rich and some of them, eventually, became powerful and respected men. These thoughts came to Manny unbidden when he saw the truck. Manny knew it was Reina and Goldman, the former his lover, the latter his boss, and both of them harping on the prohibition of alcohol being the same as the prohibition of cannabis and other drugs.

There were the stories, too, that flew through Manny's mind. The Aguilar family bootlegger, Manny's great great uncle, who got a bullet graze across the bottom of his belly while running from the cops. *How's the king of the bootleggers? They almost made me the queen of the bootleggers. La Reina.* The family joke, playing in Manny's mind. Ghost words, gossip from dead lips about those who had died before them. It was the old truck sitting in the front yard of the ranch house, he told himself. The face of it staring past him in the still, bright day. The dark radiator grill like a fencer's mask with crab's eyes poking out on either side, those empty sockets where the headlamps had been, dull and silvery, scoured by sun and wind since who knew when. Maybe it had belonged to a bootlegger. His thoughts veered off to death and wounding. To images of Donald Donahue.

Manny stopped in front of the tin-roofed porch. The screen door was closed but what door there was behind it had been left open. A faint draft of air came from inside and, with it, an odor that spoke of habitation. Manny heard the sound of footsteps and a red faced white man with wooly gray hair and a beard swung open the screen door and walked soundlessly out on the shaded ground under the porch and stood there, looking like both a king and a servant, the vagrant, flaring, gray-green rakes of young fan palms sprouting from oxidized aluminum garbage cans on either side of him like the armrests of a throne.

The conversation was pretty much routine to start. Directions to Charley Bell Pass, and so on. When the talk turned to drug smuggling and border crossers, the man claimed the crossers came out of the mountains behind him and he'd given them water at times. The Goldwater Bombing Range was not far north of this place and the man claimed the military lit the way for drug smugglers with giant lights from the sky. It was all connected, the man said, and he looked down toward the highway, lost in the distance, and said there was a devil on eighty-five.

When Manny asked about the devil the man's eyes wandered away and came back to Manny's face and the man said he'd meant that the whole thing was tied together by alignments of the government and the drug smugglers. Then he sheared off into talk about the story told in the Torah, without naming the Torah, or the Bible, and he spoke on the notion that aliens from space brought people to earth as a colony, and that the old books were a code describing it, and, certainly, they had their purposes, these people from space, and they carried on having them, and there would soon be a showing of these purposes, seeing as how the space people were about due for a visit to the petri dish they'd made of the planet.

When the man could see Manny wasn't buying the story of the old books as a tale of seedlings from space he stopped talking about it and Manny opened a badge case and identified himself as a PI. The man showed no fear but Manny noticed the man's body go rigid in the process of claiming he'd never seen the women in the photographs Manny put in front of him.

As for the black pistol tucked in Manny's belt, the man gave no indication he'd ever noticed it.

When Manny bid him a good day, a clear light came to the man's eyes and he made a short speech, seemingly meant to be affirmative, delivered as a testament without apparent context, but for the fact the old man may have noticed Manny seemed to be a Mexican-American who had the look of someone who had done violence and known horror.

"Let me tell you something," the old man said. "I have been to war, not as a fighting man but as a kind of witness, and I have seen Mexican-American boys dead on metal tables, under the ceiling of an Army tent, under an American flag pinned to its insides. I have seen the priest at two o'clock in the morning, a tired slob, awakened from his bed, come to give the last rites, his olive drab fatigue jacket open to his white undershirt, glasses falling off his nose, rosary slung in shambles from his neck, that jilted cross still hanging on and sticking in his chest. Those boys are in every little cemetery in every little town in the west. And you know, for the rest of them, nobody came in the night and said anything. Nobody said anything for about ten years, come to think of it." The man shook his wooly gray head. "Bad stuff. But it's nothing compared to what's coming. They put us here to see how we'd do and we did wrong. There are too many of us. We turned Eden into Hell—"

"You're sure you've never seen these women or this man before?" Manny said, shuffling the photographs of Evelyn Antone and the Donahues, holding the photos up for the old man to see.

The old man spread his hands out, showing his palms. "We turned Eden into Hell and we'll suffer the consequences," he said. "We took the earth's medicine and turned it into poison."

Manny put the photographs back in the folder. He turned and began walking away. The old man followed him to the dam that went across the wash outside the house.

"There's going to be cleaning of the petri dish," the old man was saying as Manny started threading his way across the top of the narrow dam. "There are too many of us."

Manny cleared the far edge of the dam and started the half-mile walk back to his truck, seeing images of dead teenagers on metal tables, and thinking again about Donny Donahue. When he had nearly reached the truck he saw a kid sitting on a camo green quad up where the dirt road, wretched with washboard, topped a hill. The kid looked in Manny's direction for a while and then he looked away. Manny got in his truck and turned it around, starting in the kid's direction. The kid drove his quad off into the desert as if he had some purpose there.

Manny thought about following the punk and demanding to know what he was doing, watching like some little *halcon*. But there was no reason, and Manny didn't want to go to Charley Bell Pass anymore. He wanted to go back to Tucson and forget about finding out who shot Evelyn Antone. Guilt was guilt. Dead was dead. To hell with it.

When he got down near highway 85 his cell phone picked up a signal and beeped. Manny pulled over on the shoulder of the dirt road, sat in the silence of a dead and windless late afternoon, and listened to the message. Somehow, Reina had read, tapped and talked her way into believing that William Walker had been a CIA agent in Latin America.

"Yeah, Manny, he was a spook, a sneaky pete, or whatever else they called them back in the day. But here's the other news," Reina said, when she answered his call. "Johnny Oaks got back to me. He attended Evelyn Antone's funeral at Sells. He didn't ask permission but nobody challenged him. He told me he saw a couple of guys the two of you didn't get around to—Joaquin and Chester Antone, Lois and Evelyn's brothers."

Manny thought about it for a minute. "Evelyn told us Joaquin was dead."

"Yeah," Reina snickered. "Oaks said you'd remember."

"Go ahead, Reina," Manny said, "make fun of me. You're right and Oaks is right, I didn't follow up on those guys."

"You've been kind of busy, honey. I'm sorry. I couldn't help but laugh. When will I see you?"

"I'll call you back and tell you after I try to call Chester Antone," Manny said. "I got his cell phone number from Evelyn. How did you find out Walker was CIA?"

"I checked with Latin American newspaper people where he'd filed stories, I called human rights organizations, stuff like that."

"So you're not sure."

"I'm as sure as I can be, Manny. The guy showed up in Latin America in 1970 and it's pretty clear he came there from Vietnam. They know that about him. He said he'd been a reporter there, too. Nobody ever saw a story he filed from Vietnam."

"A lot of people think there's a CIA agent under every bush," Manny said.

"I know that, Manny," Reina said. "That's why I spent hours and hours checking with all kinds of smart newspaper people in different countries."

"Okay."

"Okay and thank you, Reina," Reina said.

"I'll go with it. I'll look at him. I'll call you and let you know when I'm getting back. Uh, love you."

"Yes you do," Reina said.

***

Chester Antone's voice was quiet and confident, the voice of a man who was accustomed to talking to strangers. Manny offered his condolences on the death of Chester's sister and briefly explained himself, suspecting Chester would swear at him and hang up. After all, Manny had shot the husband of Chester's other dead sister.

"I'll talk to you," Chester said. "I work security at the Golden Ha:san Casino. You passed it on your way into Ajo. It's right there on 86, a mile and a half from Why. I'll be here until ten."

Manny told Chester he'd be there in about two hours and drove into Ajo. He ate dinner at the 100 Estrella Restaurant and set out for Why and beyond, raising an open hand in greeting to the white PCSD trucks parked in the little triangle of roads at the bottom of town.

***

The Golden Ha:san was small, for a casino. It served as a gas station and convenience mart as much as anything, but half of the building was dedicated to rows of slot machines. Manny went into that half of the building. The place sold no alcohol. There were a couple of players visible, listlessly stuffing nickels into the machines. There was a woman in the back of the room, standing behind a window for changing money. Then there was Chester Antone, a very big guy, just inside the door on Manny's left. The two of them stepped outside.

"Yeah, I was a janitor at the high school," Chester said, in response to Manny's comment that that his sister Evelyn had said he was a janitor. "Kind of a security guy over there, too. I was in the military police in the Army. I retired from the school system. This," he tipped his head back at the door behind him, "gives me something to do. I got a daughter in college. She needs things."

"What does Joaquin do?" Manny asked.

Chester looked down at Manny, his eyes crinkled up, and he smiled. "Joaquin's older than the rest of us kids. He's from our dad's first marriage. He's Sonoran O'odham. You know what I mean?"

Manny shook his head and waited. Clearly, this whole thing

with the Antone boys was becoming a voyage of discovery.

"He was born on the Mexican side of the nation—at home, not in a hospital. He can't get a birth certificate so he couldn't be enrolled as a tribal member here in the States—so he's got no American citizenship. He's happy on the Sonoran side but when he has to come over here, he just comes through at the Gate. You know the Gate?"

Manny shook his head again.

"The San Miguel Gate at Sells. It's comes from El Bajio on the Sonoran side. Technically, Joaquin would be an illegal alien if he went off the reservation on this side. We don't worry about it here. Blame the Treaty of Guadalupe Hidalgo." Chester had a grin simmering now. Suddenly, he went quiet and shrugged, going back into silence until he nearly disappeared. "Nice night," he said, finally, looking out over his tribe's desert in dusk's last dark light. Purple, going to black.

"Why would Evelyn tell me Joaquin was dead?" Manny asked.

Chester showed no surprise, but he gave the question a moment's thought. "I think I just I told you," he said. "It's easier than talking about Joaquin to somebody from the outside. She was pretty high strung, Evelyn. She probably didn't trust you guys. You represent federal authority to her. About once a year, I go over and drive Joaquin and his wife up to Phoenix. We kind of coast through the Border Patrol checkpoints. I bought him a Stetson hat up there one time. He liked that hat. See how it is?" Chester tipped his head a little sideways and looked at Manny with an expression as kind as any good cop telling a little kid he couldn't jaywalk.

"I can see why Evelyn might say Joaquin was dead," Manny said, not because he believed or disbelieved it. "What does Joaquin do over there?" he asked, for the second time.

"He's an old cowboy," Chester said. "He's got some cattle and he and his wife keep a garden going. They're traditional people. Good people."

"Can you help me get in touch with him?"

"You want to see if my sixty-year old brother killed both his

99

sisters?" Chester folded his arms. Big arms. He looked down at Manny. "The tribal CI's checked it out. Everybody knows family members are the first suspects. I've been cleared. Joaquin's been cleared. The cops have been all over the rez. I live a long way from my sisters—and the TO police in Sells. My wife and I built a house just a few miles from this casino. The cops called us the night Lois was killed. They were at our door at 8 o'clock the next morning. Same thing with Evelyn. Get the TO CI's reports if you don't believe it. This is professional law enforcement out here."

"Like I said when I called you, I've got a problem," Manny said, "because of that shooting, that accident. We all want the same outcome, but they won't talk to me. Thank you for talking to me. Who would kill your sisters?"

"I don't know," Chester said. He looked down, his arms still crossed. "But they'll find out who did it, sooner or later. My sisters were just regular people." He lifted his head and looked Manny in the face.

Chapter Twelve

Manny sat in his truck in the dimly lit parking lot outside the casino and called Reina. "I got a scheduling problem. I just talked to Chester Antone. He works just outside of Why. I'm ruling out the Antone brothers. That leaves me here with William Walker next on the list. I should stay in Ajo at least another night."

"Jeff wants you back, Manny," Reina said. "He's got a bunch of work for you. He's picked up a murder and what's looking like a case that's good for arguing entrapment. He's working late. He just texted me here."

"I'll see you in three hours," Manny said, happy to be headed home to his lover—and to see what she'd found out about William Walker, Ajo's news reporter at large.

***

It was all hands on deck at the Goldman Law Firm the next morning. More papers than words were exchanged. In Manny's case, a stack of police reports and witness statements which Manny read, compared, highlighted, and wrote up for inconsistencies. Following that, he was on the phone to witnesses, arranging interviews. After that, he was headed out the door to start the actual interviews—the first interview being at a bar, the environment where the witness stated she "spent most of her time and felt most comfortable."

When the work let up, Reina showed him her email correspondence with Latin American newspaper people and human rights violations investigators. William Walker had lived in some hot areas in Latin America, places few Americans ever read about, where events took place that few Americans ever read about.

He'd begun filing stories from Uruguay in 1970, when the CIA and the AID were involved in training police in torture techniques. He had been in Chile from 1971 until 1973, when Pinochet overthrew Allende—with CIA assistance. There, Walker's byline appeared on articles discussing agricultural development.

In 1979, when the Sandinistas overthrew Somoza, stories with the Walker byline began showing up in Honduras, next door to Nicaragua. And so it went until 1990, when his last story was filed, from inside Nicaragua, the year the Sandinistas were defeated in the national elections.

"You know what's weird?" Reina said, when she had shown Manny the last of the correspondence. "There was a William Walker who was a filibuster."

"I'm listening," Manny said, sensing he was about to get a history lesson from Reina.

"Be careful, Manny. You could learn something here. Walker was a five foot, two-inch tall gifted kid from an upper class family in Nashville. He was both a lawyer and a doctor. Back in 1850, he got some guys together and invaded Mexico. He invaded Latin American countries three or four times. He was hauled into American courts for violation of US neutrality laws and policies but he got let off. Then came a cruel irony, Manny. In the mood for one?"

"No," Manny said.

"I *always* am." Reina said, clasping her hands together and giving Manny a starry-eyed look. Which he returned with a scowl. "Now, the general rationale for all this invading was, hey, make it like Texas because Anglo Americans and Latinos in Texas banded together to fight for independence from Mexico back in the days of the Alamo. This invading was known as filibustering in Walker's day.

"So, Willie Walker got control of Nicaragua when they were having a civil war and one side called him in to help. Then he got crosswise with the business interests of another American, Cornelius Vanderbilt, and got kicked out. By that time, he'd already driven the Nicaraguans nuts because slavery was illegal there and he made it legal—and he made English the official language of, get this—Nicaragua," Reina paused to make the crazy sign by circling her forefinger rapidly over her head. "He then tried one last time to retake Nicaragua, got snagged by the British Navy, and, because the English had their own scams going in the region and didn't want competition, they turned Walker over to the Hondurans, who executed his tiny ass."

"Our Walker is just a guy with the wrong name," Manny said.

"Yeah. Infamous. Maybe it sold newspapers. So now what?"

"I investigate Ajo's William Walker."

"How?"

"I can't do remote surveillance from a vehicle. Somebody would notice me. I'll bug his house. I'll put a GPS on his car. See if I can get his phone records. I'll investigate him."

"You'd need to be in his house to bug it. He's far away from these murders. Bottom line, yeah, he's a suspicious character, but so what? That's half the people anywhere. Why take these risks, Manny?"

"Instinct. Like it? You're the one who pushes feelings around here."

"We either *push feelings*, as you put it, or they push us. I know where this is coming from."

Manny gave her the cop look, expressionless, dead eyes set back under somewhat protruding supraorbital ridges. "Don't say it, Reina."

"I won't say *your grandmother* if you don't say *push feelings*. How's that? Now, back to taking risks that would get your PI license pulled if you got caught—not to mention getting tangled up with a guy who either was or is now a CIA agent."

"I'll be careful," Manny said.

***

Manny was bent over under a lampshade in the dark living room of William Walker's little house on the hill, just across the street from the Curley School, when the old man told him not to move. Manny had no idea how Walker had got there. After Manny was sitting cross legged on the floor, facing him, fingers locked together on top of his head, the old man began to speak.

"What's this about?" Walker said.

Manny didn't answer.

"If I have to, I can find out everything about you," Walker said. "Now, why me? Think I'm running around killing girls on the reservation?"

Walker was sitting in a straight backed Mexican chair, holding his gun up sideways, and Manny knew the old man could point it and pull the trigger fast. This was what he had seen in the dream of a figure holding something up—a gun.

"A gift from my government," Walker said, noticing Manny's stare. "Not a mark on it—no serial numbers, no proof marks, no maker's name. It's a nude Browning, as they say. It's not that it's untraceable—it never existed in the first place. Now, I'd hate to have to shoot you with it, but I will if you try to jump me. Tell me your story and do it damn quick, boy."

"I knew you weren't the way you presented yourself here in Ajo," Manny said. "I was in army intelligence during my enlistment. I worked around people like you. I got suspicious. I had to check you out. I'm a PI, like I told you. I gave you my real name. I used to be a detective with the Pima County Sheriff's Department. I wanted to know if you had any connection to the murders of Lois Donahue and Evelyn Antone."

"Bullshit."

"Beck, the drug counselor, or somebody, wrote the name 'Walker' on the sheath of a knife he left for me with a neighbor. I could show you the knife. It's in my briefcase in my truck."

"So's a handgun, most likely," Walker said. "So are you Nancy Drew, or somethin'? Seen a name on a knife? I never owned a knife I gave to Beck so I didn't write my name on it. People like me don't write our names on our underwear and stuff like that, son. If Beck wrote that name, you should ask him. You knew I'd been some kind of intelligence guy and you had a name on the belt loop of a knife. That's *all*? You're not stupid—well, maybe you are, but no PI sneaks into a man's house and, I'm guessing by the little thing with wires you got hanging out of your shirt pocket, tries to bug it, without a better pair of reasons than that."

"Beck died," Manny said. "He died up in Washington State. Call my boss's office in Tucson," Manny said. "Goldman Law Firm. Reina can explain it." This was a low point for Manny. So many things he'd never live down. So many things. It was a 'just shoot me' moment but Manny had already been shot once or twice in his life and had never considered it a viable alternative, even before he had been shot. He only hoped Reina would be in. Chances were good that she would be. It was two o'clock in the afternoon.

"Lie down, facing away from me, and spread eagle," Walker said. "When you've done that, take your cell phone off your hip and toss it toward me, real easy."

When Manny had done that, Walker checked Manny's phone. "What's your office number? Last one you dialed, right?" Walker had already figured that out.

"Yes," Manny said.

"And who's on the other end?"

"Reina," Manny said. "Her name's Reina, she's the paralegal. She can explain this."

"It really *is* his grandmother, you know," Reina said, as if explaining a child's incredible stupidity to another adult. Walker had asked her why Manny was in his house and they'd chatted a bit.

"His grandmother's spirit told him something about you, Mr. Walker. That was the kicker—he suspected you weren't what you seemed, and then there was the knife. Hey, I kidded him about the knife. I told him bugging your house was a bad idea and he could lose his PI license. But go with his grandmother's spirit on this one. He has a higher form of intuition, or something. I've seen it work. Native American, you know. He's part Yaqui."

"How about I just turn him over to the sheriffs so they can get him the help he so desperately needs?" Walker said, irritably. "And maybe you get yourself a support group for women who love wack jobs too much."

"How about *you* help him find out who killed those women?" Reina countered.

"Lady, you got some brass balls," Walker said.

Chapter Thirteen

Eventually, after more conversation with Reina, and a phone call or two to further verify Manny's identity and work credentials, Walker let Manny sit up in a chair.

The old man sighed. "Manny, I spent thirty years working for the United States of America. Then I retired. When I retired, I did something a lot of people in my profession never do because it's a career killer. I got married. We'd been sweethearts in college. We were true believers back then. Get married, stay married. Mortgage, two kids. Stop the Communists. But she wasn't going to marry somebody who disappeared into the third world and stayed there for years.

"We kept in touch. Her husband died. I retired. When we finally married, she got breast cancer and died—just like that. Now, I've got some friends in Virginia and D.C. and roundabout, but not many. So I'm here now. Where it's quiet, at least by my standards. This is a smuggling corridor and all. Let's say it's a lower intensity war than the other wars I'm used to." The old man smiled. "Then you came along. Now, I don't contact my former associates without a real good reason. They do not want any truck with you once you quit the company. Common sense should tell you that—and it should tell your girlfriend that, too. I'll keep my eyes and ears open around here and I'll use my contacts to get information for you—but only if you really need it. Should anybody ask, I'm only an old Ajo reporter and I don't own a gun. Got it? Because, if you blow my cover, retired or not, I can still make some calls—about you."

Manny told Walker that it sounded fair and Walker let Manny walk back out into the Arizona sunshine.

"Tell your girlfriend I said hello," Walker called, as Manny was leaving. "And your grandmother." Manny walked away down the hill. The old man's whispery laughter followed him until it vanished at some point Manny could not quite discern.

When he reached his truck, parked at the bottom of the hill, Manny noticed a kid across the street, watching him. A different kid from the one on the quad out at Charley Bell Pass, but one with the same intent. When Manny looked at him, the kid shifted his body insolently and stared in a different direction. Manny wondered if the kid belonged to Walker. Maybe that was how Walker had managed to sneak up on him.

Manny's next thought had to do with where he'd first seen a *halcon*—and that was at the desert rat's—the man who knew the space people were coming back to check on their science project. For all Manny knew at this point in his day, the guy might be right. Nevertheless, now that he was still alive, Manny decided he'd have to ask at least one more question before he left town.

***

"A desert rat out Charley Bell Pass way, huh?" Chuck Dacey said, leaning back and crossing his arms. The Copper News offices were close to closing but Dacey was relaxed and attentive as usual. "I can't help you on that one. Check with the Border Patrol. They get everywhere on those quads, sooner or later."

Manny had no contacts with the Border Patrol. He headed out of Ajo, stopping at the little triangle of roads at the bottom of town to ask the sheriff's officers about the desert rat. No help there. As Manny got his truck up to speed on the dark strip of highway that led out of town he wondered at himself for never having asked the desert rat, the hermit, for his name.

***

Sylvia Mendez was late for work at the cafe and art gallery in Sells. She'd driven in from the western part of town in late morning, passing a bored patrol officer who slumped in his cruiser under an anemic, lonely mesquite tree.

Her hair was still wet from a morning shower and her eyes

were glued to the asphalt as she made her way to the glass doors of the café and came through it, tottering a little. She was overweight and the doctors kept telling her she was coming on to a good case of diabetes, ushered along by a six pack of cheap beer every night—or was it a twelve-pack? She hadn't been counting.

The glass door connecting to the art gallery was locked. That surprised her. Albert was never late. He was too fussy for that. All up in his blue button down shirts, Sylvia thought. Mr. big shot art dealer. Some days she wished the crossed pistols tattooed on her chest were real.

Albert made a point of locking the glass door to the art gallery and there was an alarm in there that he didn't trust her to operate. But he should have arrived by now. She began brewing coffee. The hours crept by. She was bored out of her skull but grateful, at the same time, that there were no customers. Then the cops rolled up in front of the place with their lights on. She eventually learned that the patrol officer sitting under the mesquite tree had driven by the back of the place and noticed the rear door ajar. He'd called out, stepped inside the stock room, and found Albert Azarola shot dead. Sylvia's first thought was that the cops would be all over her ass again, asking questions, like they were when Lois got killed, and she wouldn't get another beer until the middle of the freaking night.

***

Manny waited until he'd turned onto state route 86, his truck now pointed east, toward Tucson, before he made the call.

"Reina," he said, when she answered. "Thanks for getting me out of that one. You were right about bugging Walker's house, and I apologize."

"Well, I guess," Reina said.

"Do me a favor? Don't rub it in."

"You almost got killed."

"I knew you were going to say that."

"Do you think you can drive back home to a woman and a cat

and a dog and even a lawyer who loves you without getting into any more trouble—*today*, at least?"

Manny assured Reina that he could, indeed, do that. But then he reached the western outskirts of Sells and he thought, since he was already there, in Sells, why not just cruise by the café on his way through town and put a cop's eyeball on that café manager who had called the TO police when he and Oaks had been there. Just see what the guy's affect was like. Manny knew very well that the FBI and the TO CI's had been all over this manager because Lois worked with him every day. Outside of family, a coworker, especially a male coworker, had to be cleared. Manny eased off State Route 86 and eased into Sells.

He saw the flashing lights well before he reached the shopping center. Cops all over the place at the café, which was situated at one end of the U-shaped collection of stores forming the shopping center, with the parking lot in the open space in the middle of the U.

Manny's conversation with Reina about staying out of trouble was still fresh in his mind, along with a slight case of the shakes, which had set in after looking down the muzzle of William Walker's really cool, classic, Belgian made, nine-millimeter Browning High Power. And, Manny had an information source that might be able to give him the story in real time. Manny spun his truck around and blew town, stopping when he was safely over the big hill east of Sells and placing a call to Coyote Bob. It was quitting time, five o'clock. Bob would be home from his art teaching job—toking up, probably.

"Uhhh, no," Bob said, when he answered Manny's call. "I don't know what's going on out there. Sasha's still on her way home from work. I'll call her and get back to you." His voice sounded like it was coming from somewhere inside a nasal cavity the size of Colossal Cave, a local Tucson tourist attraction. Manny hung up and drove, hoping Coyote Bob wasn't too baked to follow through with a call back.

"Yeah, it's uh...that guy," Coyote Bob said, when he called back a few minutes later. "It's the art gallery manager. Somebody killed him and robbed the place."

Manny thanked Bob and kept rolling for Reina's house. Then he stopped again and made another call.

"Buy you dinner?" he asked Reina.

"Let's eat in," Reina said. "We've got food, I can cook it, and I have a man living with me who gets guns pointed at him every time he leaves the house."

"So, can I pick up anything for you on the way home?"

"Don't even start being a smartass," Reina said, and hung up.

Chapter Fourteen

"Welcome back," Goldman said to Manny, about 9:05 the next morning. "Now get to work."

Manny found himself once again in a routine of comparing police reports to witness statements, followed by witness interviews. When he had done all he could do for the day, he took a deep breath and called the hospital where Donald Donahue was still recovering. Manny apologized and repeated an explanation that Goldman had made clear in a previous conversation with Donald. That explanation being that the prosecution and the TO police had not notified Donald Donahue's defense team in a timely fashion when charges had been dropped.

"I know it was an accident, what you did," Donald said to Manny. "I want to get out of here so I can help take care of Jonas and go back to work."

"Did you hear about Lois's old boss being murdered?" Manny asked. "Albert Azarola?"

"Yeah, I heard about that."

"Do you think that has something to do with Lois and Evelyn?"

"Sounds like somebody wanted to kill all of 'em," Donald said.

"I'm going to keep looking for whoever killed Lois and your sister-in-law, Evelyn. Goldman and Reina want me to keep looking, too. Is that okay with you?"

"Did you find anybody?"

"I eliminated a couple of people I suspected. Let me know if you hear anything."

"Reina," Jeff called through the half open door of his office, "I've got Tracy Engelbart and her father coming in at three. Let me know when they arrive."

Presently, a dignified looking twenty-something came

through the door of the Goldman Law Firm, accompanied by a haunted looking older man who was obviously her father. Reina showed Tracy Engelbart and her father into Goldman's office. Goldman showed the pair out again a half-hour later. He then stalked back to the door of his office, leaned on the door frame, and began remarking on his encounter. Manny tried to ignore him while reviewing a faxed ME's report on Lois Donahue. Reina listened with interest.

"The Tucson Police enjoy a weak city council, a strong public relations department, and an entrenched county attorney who everybody votes for because she's a Democrat. She's got a team of prosecutors who do nothing but take money off people who get caught using marijuana. It's a machine.

"They'll throw multiple felony charges on anybody who gets caught with pot—and, in these conservative times, nobody hires anybody who has a felony record—so that makes it real easy for the prosecutors to take a twenty-year-old pharmacy student from the University of Arizona—who's got four pot plants in her closet—for a few thousand dollars to get those felony charges reduced to misdemeanors. That money simultaneously pays the expenses of the local criminal justice establishment, justifies its existence, and makes it look good because it's a self-supporting engine that generates its own dollars, thereby requiring fewer monies from the citizenry—at least from the citizenry's limited perspective. Actually, we're all getting screwed on taxes by the drug wars.

"You could never be a pharmacist with a drug felony conviction on your record. You could be an Arizona State Attorney General with a record of securities law violations, campaign finance law violations—and even a record for leaving the scene of a traffic accident, which was witnessed by FBI investigators—but not a pot smoking pharmacist. Not in Arizona."

"So what did you tell Tracy to do?" Reina asked.

"I advised Tracy to plead to the misdemeanors and pay the money—because they're holding her future for ransom. She won't need me to help her plead—but that's part of the prosecutorial plan—make defense attorneys useless against the war on drugs, which is propped up by the Arizona voters, some of the nastiest old hicks you've ever seen, people who drink alcohol every night." He turned as if to disappear into his office and then turned back, holding up one finger in a theatrical gesture. "And I quote Charles Bowden: 'It was *never* about drugs.'"

After that, Goldman finally did disappear into his office, followed by Reina's amused gaze and Manny's impassive one.

"You know," Reina said, addressing Manny, "I knew a guy who worked for the Cochise County Attorney's office—a lawyer. His sole job was collecting his county's share of drug forfeitures. The war on drugs is pathetic. What are you reading?"

"The Medical Examiner's report on Lois Donahue," Manny said. "The fire burned all of Lois's soft tissue, so no DNA there. The techs sampled the femur and the teeth. They cleaned the outside of her femur, powdered up the bone and tooth matrix, and did some kind of specialized 'decalcification' extraction and concentration. Then they got the 'STR' typing results. Says here that stands for 'Short Tandem Repeat,' and it's the same kind of results they'd get from sampling blood, saliva, skin cells, or whatever, for DNA. Then they matched it up with Evelyn's DNA, eliminating pretty much everybody but Evelyn's sister, Lois," Manny looked up and locked eyes with Reina. "And there's a one in three chance Lois was murdered over drugs."

"Money, love, or drugs," Reina said, "the top three motives for murder. Take the money out of drugs, Manny—dammit. Al Capone was out of business the day after Prohibition ended."

The phone rang, interrupting what was promising to be a pretty good quarrel over what to do about a multi-billion dollar a year industry. Reina listened, eyes brightening.

"Sure," she said, finally. "We'd love to see those tapes." Reina listened and talked and scribbled, eventually closing the conversation and hanging up the phone. "Donald Donahue phoned up the other barista," Reina said, looking across the room at Manny. "Sylvia Mendez. Seems Sylvia's got some CCTV tapes from the Ban 'eldag Cafe. Want to go pick them up?"

***

Finding Sylvia Mendez's house on the western outskirts of Sells wasn't the easiest task Manny had ever accomplished but he got it done. He was rewarded with a worn cardboard box half filled with dusty video tapes from the old fashioned CCTV cameras that guarded the café. Sylvia had found them one day when Albert wasn't around. She'd taken them home, planning to record horror films over them. She didn't know why Albert had saved them—or why he'd changed the CCTV tapes, instead of letting one tape play through and record over at twenty-four hour intervals.

"Maybe he was stupid," Sylvia opined.

Why hadn't Sylvia turned the tapes over to the TO cops? Because then she'd have to explain why she had them in the first place. Cops were such a pain in the ass. Always asking questions. Manny asked Sylvia questions about Lois and Albert and invited her to speculate on why Lois was murdered—and then Evelyn. Sylvia described Albert as "a dick," and stated that Lois was nice but she hardly knew her because they worked different shifts, and who knew why any of it happened, anyway.

"Did the cops say anything about the surveillance tape that was running when this incident with Albert happened?" Manny asked.

"Yeah," Sylvia said. "They asked me where it was four of five times is all."

"So they didn't find it at the crime scene? It wasn't in the machine?"

"Guess not," Sylvia said. "You'd have to be kind of a dumbass to cap somebody and leave a surveillance tape for the cops. I think I saw that whole tape machine on the floor in there—all busted up. That's what I'd do. Wouldn't you?"

Sylvia was into her fourth beer when Manny left.

***

"Are you coming over tonight or are you staying at your bachelor pad?" Reina asked, when Manny answered his cell phone. He'd been at his little house on 15ᵗʰ Street since five p.m., watching crude, low resolution images of the Ban el'dag Café and art gallery.

He glanced at his watch. Nine p.m. "I'll be right over."

***

Manny spent every spare moment over the next several days watching the tapes. When he'd seen them all and had taken notes, he asked his boss and his coworker to sit down with him and talk it over.

"I saw your friend George on those tapes," Manny said, nodding at Reina.

"What was he doing?" Reina said, unconsciously giving him the full benefit of how beautiful her eyes were, now that they had gone very wide.

"He knew Albert," Manny said. "There's video of him standing around the back door of the gallery with Albert."

"But does that mean anything?" Goldman said, staring offhandedly across the room.

"Other than uniformed delivery people and the baristas, Lois included, George was the only person on those tapes who knew Albert well enough to hang around by the stockroom door in the back of that place," Manny said. "I want to check it out."

"And you don't want him to know, do you?" Reina said. "And I guess we aren't going to turn the tapes over the proper authorities?"

"Sylvia Mendez will deny she ever had those tapes if we turn them over to TO police. Donny will deny he ever called us and he entrusted this information to us. He trusts us more than he trusts his tribe's police force," Manny said.

"You've committed a crime if you don't turn those tapes over," Goldman said. "I'm sure you know that. I will deny any knowledge of this if I am asked about it. I have no choice. You're on your own. Are we clear?"

"Yes," Manny said.

"How are you going to check this guy out?" Goldman asked. "I can't ask the courts for any actions or permissions regarding anything related to these murders. Stay off this George person's property. I heard about your close call with a Mr. Walker out there in Ajo." Goldman and Reina exchanged *simpatico* responsible adult caregiver nods. "And please do not consider hacking his phone records," Goldman continued. "That is a felony under the Telephone Records and Privacy Protection Act of 2006—signed into federal law by The Gimp."

"That's Dubya," Reina said sharply. "Not The Gimp."

"Right," Goldman said, pointing a finger at Reina. "My mistake. The Gimp was in a box in Maynard's pawn shop— Tarantino film."

"That's okay," Reina said. "I get it mixed up all the time."

Manny watched Reina's body do great things to a black sweater and a tight plaid skirt as she lifted her shoulders, threw her hands out, and shrugged helplessly.

"And the felony charges for hacking go straight through the hacker and right up the line to whoever ordered it," Goldman said, "—unless you're our government."

"Or somebody else's," Reina said. She turned to Manny. "I'll go run George's background. Want to come?"

They left Jeff Goldman alone to get back to his work and came out to Reina's desk.

After twenty minutes, Reina said, "Nothing. I'm practically snow blind from the utter vanilla of George's recorded life experience."

"What's his military record?" Manny asked.

"Something about the 88th Support Battalion in Korea, around the time of the Korean War," Reina replied. "Ready to accept the possibility that George is just a guy with some very ordinary reason to know that art dealer—like maybe an interest in *art*? Why don't I just mention it to him and watch his response? I see him once or twice a week at meditation."

"Why don't I try our friend Walker out in Ajo?" Manny said. "This would be a good time to check on him—see if he's afraid of us."

"I like the way you think," Reina said. "In spite of the insane mortal danger you're asking for by having any contact with that guy—so I'll call him myself."

Manny watched her riffle through her cell phone and call a number. She had a brief, apparently pleasant conversation, and then hung up.

"He'll call us back in an hour," she said. "Nice old murderous spook that he is."

***

Walker, true to his word, called back in an hour.

"Mind if I put you on speaker phone?" Reina asked, knowing she was probably pushing the envelope with a person who had supposedly spent most of his life whispering and sneaking around. Reina listened to Walker's response and then handed her cell phone over to Manny. Manny took the phone and turned away, identifying himself. "Good old boy network," Reina groused, to no one in particular, and waited for Manny to hang up and report his findings.

"Your friend George was in the Counter Intelligence Corps in the Army," Manny said, after he had bid Walker goodbye. "He was in the Korean War."

"What's the Counter Intelligence Corps?" Reina asked. "Wait! Google knows!"

After a moment of wide-eyed searching, she said, "Oh, an *Army* spook agency. Fancy that. They snuck Klaus Barbie out of Germany after WW II. Nice work, guys. Korean War was the last time they were in action—oops, I was wrong. They just renamed themselves after the Korean War and blew our tax dollars spying on social activists for the next thirty years. So does that necessarily make George a bad person, Manny? He was in the Army decades ago—in a war. He didn't stay in the Army. I know for a fact that he's a retired accountant and businessman. What do you think?"

"Did he ever mention his military service to you?" Manny asked. "Did you ever hear him mention it to anybody?"

"No," Reina said. "And so what? We don't sit around our sangha telling war stories."

"You don't sit on your sangha telling war stories?"

"We don't sit *on* our sangha, Manny. Sangha means 'community.'"

"Why don't you just say 'community'?"

"Why don't you get stuffed?"

"I'm going to track George's movements for a while. Walker said there's some reason to believe George is doing something suspicious. Walker wouldn't, maybe couldn't, say anything more."

Reina could see Manny had his cop look on. "Do what you have to do, Manny. You showed me the tapes from the Ban 'eldag. George obviously knew Albert, the dead guy, and knew him well."

"When does your meditation group meet?"

"This evening at six," Reina said. "I'm going—so I can have the equanimity to deal with my crazy boyfriend. George should be there, too."

Chapter Fifteen

Manny parked on the side of the street opposite the meditation center, a white stucco home tucked away on a residential street near the University of Arizona. The building had a flat roof and a half-circle driveway. An island of decorative cactus, flowers, and a mesquite tree filled the space between the street side of the driveway and the street itself. Manny noted a mailbox topping a post, painted with flowers and its door hanging open like a tongue.

Manny watched as people began arriving for the 6 p.m. meditation session. He saw Reina pull up in her black Honda. She took no notice of him and went inside. A minute later, an older van pulled up and George got out. Tall, lean, the hairs of his eyebrows pointing in opposite directions like sabers, George made for the door of the center, paused to take off his shoes, and disappeared inside.

Manny waited fifteen minutes for stragglers, then got out of his truck, slipped across the street, opened the unlocked door of George's van, leaned under the dashboard, and shoved a GPS tracking device into the van's on-board diagnostic port. The device could remain there indefinitely, recharging itself on George's car battery. Manny got back in his truck and checked his cell phone to make sure the device had sent him his initial text message. It had.

***

"So, Jeff, how'd you do with that single mother caught with a carload of cannabis?" Reina asked her employer as he entered the office late the following morning, wearing his court clothes.

"She got three years. They wanted to give her five. Another case where the grandparents raise the kid, although the grandparents would be raising the kid anyway if she were a drug addict—which she is not," Goldman said, taking a chair beside Reina's desk. "These cartel guys are good manipulators. This girl was at a party and a guy talked her into smuggling a load. All she knew was the first name the guy gave her and two cell phone numbers—one to call on the Mexican side when she got there—in her own car—and one to call when she got the load across."

"We almost never see methamphetamine."

"It's easier to hide so it doesn't get busted as much, people make that stuff domestically as well, and, let's face it, pot's the most popular drug in America. Pot's ninety percent of the federal busts for smuggling. Where's our investigator?"

"Out buying camera stuff," Reina said. "Now he's got it in his head that some hermit outside of Ajo might be part of the Ban 'eldag murders."

"And so they have come to be called," Goldman said. "Two out of three employees at the same place of business, murdered at different times. And an additional murder of the sister of one of those employees. I'm surprised the whole thing hasn't been solved. The social connections and the motives have to be there. Manny was looking at George. Now he's looking at a *hermit*? Is he okay?"

Reina's eyes clouded. "Yeah, he's okay." She recovered herself and shook her head. "He's okay... I guess. If the FBI and TO police hadn't failed to solve these crimes—like you said, three murders that scream 'Connected!' in a likewise connected, tribal community—then Manny's actions would just seem so, so crazy, Jeff. But I talk to Coyote Bob and Sasha out on the rez. They know a staffer at TO police headquarters. The TO cops are frustrated, clueless. I don't have anybody who's close to the FBI, so who knows what they have—but there haven't been any arrests. What Manny's got is George all over those café tapes and now this hermit with what Manny says was obvious liar's body language when Manny showed this guy the photographs of Evelyn and Lois. I say go with it—and Manny will—of course."

***

"So how's this going to work again?" Reina asked Manny, when he returned to Goldman's office an hour later.

Manny took a chair by Reina's desk, its legs scraping on Goldman's oak floor. "Tomorrow morning, I'm going to drive out to the desert around Ajo, find a place to park the truck, and hike up to a ridge that overlooks this guy's little ranch house. Then I'm going to set up a camera and hike back out."

"What do you hope to find out from doing that?"

"How he moves, for one thing," Manny said. "I didn't see any vehicles around his place or even a road leading in. He's got to get in and out of there for supplies. I don't have his picture. I'll try to get an image of him if he steps outside. I checked with a contact who has access to Arizona driver license records. This guy has no driver's license. I'd like to talk with the shuttle service in Ajo. They run people to Phoenix and Tucson. They're right on the main drag in Ajo. I don't want to let them know I'm looking if I can't show them a picture of the guy and they're the ones with the law on their side. They don't have to tell me anything about their passengers."

"How long a hike?" Reina asked.

"I'm guessing four miles in, four out."

"So you sneak in there on foot. Border Patrol is always out there, aren't they? And we know they have spotters up on the high hills. So do the cartels."

"Yeah, somebody will spot me, that's a real good bet."

"So, what are you wearing?" Reina said.

Manny glanced at his pants. "Right now? You mean, for underwear? Are you talking we slip away? Get out of the office?"

"No," Reina said. "And no—but I'll take you up on that tonight, big fella. I meant on the hike."

"What? I'm wearing hiking boots, my green 5.11 tactical pants—they're nice and roomy—and my old OD Remington hunting jacket, and a boonie hat. Why?"

"Camo boonie hat?"

"Is there another kind?"

"So, Manny, you're going hiking in that desert looking like a soldier, hunter, cop, gun nut, survivalist freak, prepper, whatever?"

"People hunt out there—they have hunting seasons. You can carry weapons out there."

"Point is, Manny, you want to look harmless. Let's get you fixed up with some proper hiker's duds."

"No," Manny said. "And, what's more, *hell* no."

***

At 5:45 that evening, Manny found himself sitting in the passenger seat of Reina's car. He felt like a trapped and bitter animal. Reina was pulling into a shopping mall.

"What's this REI?" Manny asked, looking up at the sign on the building.

"It stands for 'Really Expensive Inventory,'" Reina said. "It has what you need."

Manny followed Reina into the store, noting a jumble of crap he couldn't use as he did so. One section was devoted to bicycles. Definitely not a Manny Aguilar thing. This was a place for hikers who never hunted, hikers who hated guns, hikers who weren't cops. Hikers who bought gear in loud colors that would scare horses, provoke bulls to charge, send wild animals scampering over the next ridge, and make perfect targets for anybody with a firearm.

Reina led him upstairs to the men's clothing section.

"Let's start with a new hat," she said, and took him over to a couple of racks filled with hats. Some of them looked decent— muted colors, brims that you could get out of your way when you needed to sight a rifle real fast. Hats you could crumple up and put in a pocket. Hats that would hold water so you could dip them into a *tinaja* and drink out of the hat if you had to.

There were no camouflage hats, however, and Manny started noticing pink hats and purple hats and lime green hats. Hats that had labels on them saying things about women's cadet hats. Striped and checkered hats. Big straw hats that would come off in the brush. Headgear for men with names like the "Marmot Shamus Hat." Manny noted that this was not a hat, but a beanie—like gangsters and college kids wore, he thought. Then there was the "Columbia Peak Ascent Peruvian Hat," another hat that wasn't a hat, but another beanie, looking to Manny like an old fashioned aviator's cap with girl's braids. He knew he was getting pissed. He knew his eyes were starting to get that dead look that preceded violence.

"Here we go," Reina said, and pulled up a big, light blue floppy hat made of ultra-lightweight nylon, sporting a colorful band sewn on the outside, displaying repeating images of a stick figure. "See how it protects the back of your neck?" She unstuck a little square of Velcro on the back of the largely shapeless hat, which hung in her hands like an exhausted fruit bat. A curtain fell from the back of the hat and spread out. Manny could see that it would work well. He didn't like the front bill. It would limit peripheral vision. Only an old lady would wear this hat, he thought. He kept that thought to himself.

"What's that design on the sweatband?" Manny said.

"This stick drawing that looks like a Rastafarian sucking a bong pipe?" Reina said, pointing at the green thread sewn in a repeating pattern.

"Yeah."

"That's Kokopeli, the flute player," Reina said. "It's a Hopi symbol having to do with crops and fertility. He used to have a visible penis but that had to be taken off once he was gathered into the pale arms of southwestern suburban culture and endlessly replicated. You're glad you have a hat like this. Try it on."

***

The next morning, Manny, looking grim, put on his hiker disguise. On top, he wore a gossamer hiking shirt with all kinds of vents and pockets, colored in a high visibility emergency-vehicle green. The worst shot in the world could not fail to hit that shirt right in the middle, Manny reflected. On his bottom, Manny sported a pair of two-tone nylon hiking shorts, colored in lighter and then darker earth tones, giving the initial impression that he had wet his pants. He already had decent hiking boots and socks. He had known, out front, that Reina couldn't screw those up. He carried a blazing blue daypack, a cheap one, with bright yellow trim. Inside it, he had two cameras, both DSLR's, both with zoom lenses. One of them, a two-thousand-dollar Nikon, a so-called prosumer camera, would shoot well in very low light.

Manny hadn't enjoyed paying for the new camera—or for the camera accessories necessary to do what he needed to do—but cameras were tools of the trade. Aside from the cameras, Manny had the usual daypack contents—mainly drinking water, essential for anybody who wanted to stay alive in the Sonoran desert.

Hikers with day packs and, especially, backpackers, wore thin or no belts. Belts interfered with the waist belts built into the packs. Manny could not safely and comfortably carry, or quickly access, his usual three-pound, belt-carried .45 automatic while wearing a day pack with a nylon waist belt just big enough to be annoying. He'd borrowed a James Bond gun from his gun loving friend, Darrell Trainor. The Walther PPKS was flat, thin, and of an elongated triangular design dating back to the 1930's. It fit in front pants pockets without showing its outline. It didn't dig into his thigh like a revolver's cylinder would—and it was not an awkward, blocky Glock, which could never be comfortably stuffed in a front pants pocket.

Manny's last, but not least, hiker's apparel item was a wooden hiking staff of the biblical variety, slight bumps running the length of it where branches had been trimmed off. The whole thing had been sprayed with a nasty plastic sealant to protect it and make it shiny. The staff was decorated with a leather strap and a large feather. He grasped it firmly in his hand and tapped his way out Reina's front door.

"Go get 'em, tiger," Reina said, giving him a friendly slap on the ass as he trundled away in his two-tone shorts.

***

Five hours later, Manny was two hours into the hike. Winter or no, the Sonoran desert got warm after you'd been hiking for a couple of hours—especially when a lot of it was up and down country, where there was as much rock as there was sand. That could be the trouble with going undercover as a hiker—you had to hike.

Hiding in plain sight, meaning broad daylight, for this mission was the sensible option. Night hiking in the Arizona desert borderlands was generally done by only four classes of people: economic migrants who were technically illegal, but seldom dangerous; drug mules, carrying sixty-pound packs of marijuana and escorted by armed cartel soldiers; and, rarely, bandits, who hoped to rob the unarmed economic migrants or even the drug smugglers. At any given time, however, the fourth and largest group out at night in these deserts was the United States Border Patrol, armed, dangerous, and no strangers to crepuscular gunfights with the cartels and the bandits.

Manny estimated he was twenty minutes from the base of the ridge backing the hermit's place when he found human remains—a skull, spine, and pelvis, scattered over the desert. He noticed scraps of clothing and the remains of a cheap backpack not unlike his own. He reminded himself not to punctuate his thoughts with profanity. He made a point of not swearing in the presence of the dead—even if he'd killed them himself. This was not something he could report. Not yet.

He went on in the blazing afternoon light, images of Reina appearing in his mind—along with images of a death map she'd shown him during an argument about immigration. The death map covered the deserts of southern Arizona. The map showed flat country in a chalky tan color and mountain ranges in a pale green the texture of alkali. Red dots sprinkled on the map represented hundreds of crosser deaths in the deadliest stretch of country in the lower 48 states. Organizations shared death maps routinely in this part of the world and the maps were always changing, but, once a death dot appeared on a death map, it stayed there. Just being out here in a vast desert could get you to thinking about the relatively small size of your personal dramas. Viewing a rotting human pelvis worked even better.

Manny's job had nothing directly to do with migrant deaths— nothing directly, but the economy and the politics of the whole country had something to do with it, indirectly. The desert and the dead and the dangers—Manny Aguilar's everyday. Lots of people's everyday—out here. He'd report the body when he got his job done. He'd reached the base of the ridge now. He took a drink of water, slid the Walther's thumb safety to the off position, and started up, picking his way through the rock.

Manny lay prone, rested, and watched the hermit's place when he reached the top of the ridge. There was no movement, just the house itself and an outbuilding about half the size of the house—big enough to garage a quad, Manny noted. Big enough to store a load of cannabis. The ruin of the Chevrolet truck, a wheelbarrow, and various construction scraps completed the picture, along with some nice Saguaros and a couple of Organ Pipe cacti. The famous Organ Pipe Cactus National Monument was just a few miles down State Route 85.

Manny had asked around and looked at county assessor's records. The hermit's name was Eugene Close. A criminal records check had revealed nothing. Manny waited for an hour, hoping Eugene might step out of the house. Eugene didn't show and Manny left his camera among the rocks, loaded with 128 gigs of memory, and hooked up to an external battery pack and an intervalometer—a timing device with such a geeky name he dared not utter it in Reina's presence for fear of reprisals. Everything was padded, and all but the lens was covered with water resistant camouflage material. He'd mounted the camera on a mini-tripod, and aimed it down at the little rancho where Eugene Close lived. In two weeks, he'd have a few thousand images—or a broken or absent camera.

Chapter Sixteen

Manny spent the next two weeks doing routine investigative work in Tucson and living his life with Reina and their two pets. He'd continued to monitor the movement of George's van via text messages sent from the GPS transmitter he'd planted. George's van hadn't left town or gone much of anywhere but to the meditation center, the grocery store, and the houses of George's friends.

***

When two weeks had gone by, Manny was back, bushwhacking the desert, wearing his two-tone shorts, his floppy hat, and carrying his wooden stick with the leather strap and the feather. This time, he carried a GPS and inputted the location of the body he'd found when he got to it. He then went up the back side of the ridge above Eugene Close's place, rested, and then watched for an hour without seeing anything or anybody.

He retrieved his camera and checked the display screen before sneaking off down the back side of the ridge. Images appeared on the screen. They'd look way better once he'd photoshopped them. The light sensitivity settings were measured in what photographers spoke of as ISO numbers. Two-thousand bucks worth of an especially fast DSLR—meaning one that could render good images in next to no light—and an approximately correct manual exposure setting would damn near give you night vision. Almost all images recorded in daylight would be useless, overexposed. Daylight wasn't generally when criminal activity happened so Manny wasn't worried. The color of the earth was tan and the sky was open. The moon was now full, and had been coming full when Manny planted the camera. Whatever outdoor movement had occurred at Eugene Close's ranch would be revealed well enough to see what was going on.

***

The Border Patrol was waiting by his truck when he got back to it. He was surprised that they hadn't been waiting for him two weeks before, when he'd gone in and planted the camera. They tried to see everything and they always had pressure sensor devices planted underground, along with motion detectors set above ground, and radar towers, and, of late, drones flying overhead, watching from the skies.

He had parked the truck on a dirt trail. He'd left a note that he was hiking, along with a couple of plastic gallon jugs of water, in case somebody needed it. Since his round trip took about six hours, he'd also buried a couple gallon jugs of water two-hundred feet from the truck, in case some crosser stole the truck and stranded him—an unlikely scenario, but possible.

Manny told the border patrol he was out hiking and doing photography. They didn't believe he was telling them the whole story, but they didn't bother to say so. There weren't any bales of dope in his truck and he was obviously a US citizen. Nevertheless, up close, Manny Aguilar didn't look like a guy who'd carry a shiny wooden hiking staff with a leather thong and a feather. Up close, Manny looked like a guy who'd be carrying what "the Pickles," the green-clad Border Patrol officers were carrying—black M4 carbines and black handguns with high capacity magazines. He gave them the GPS coordinates for the dead body and went on his way.

***

Manny showed up at Reina's house around suppertime. They cooked and ate, closely attended by the cat and the dog. Then, Manny dropped by his little house on 15th Street and began down loading the thousands of images recorded on his camera. Rather than hang around while this happened, he went back to Reina's and spent the night. He'd kept his house and he'd left his desktop computer there, even though he stayed at Reina's—a habit he'd picked up when she took him to her place to recover after he'd been thrown in a Mexican graveyard and left there for dead.

***

The next evening found Manny in his house. The place was dark, lit only by his computer screen. He dove into the world of digital image processing and came up with some pictures showing that the punk he'd seen on the quad—or another punk just like him— had visited Eugene Close two nights before with a load of something wrapped in burlap. It could only be cannabis. The kid had made several trips in and out on his quad. It appeared that Eugene assisted during the entire procedure.

Manny did not dislike the hermit, Eugene Close, but Close was violating the law and Manny wanted to know why Close had gotten nervous, suddenly, looking at photographs of Lois and Evelyn Donahue. Getting Close arrested for doing what he was doing—committing a federal crime—would position Manny to ask questions about the murdered women and give Manny a second chance, since he'd previously been defeated by Devin Woods's false confession. Officer Tellez, PCSD, Ajo Station, was only a phone call away and Manny was reaching for his cell phone when it rang.

"How's it going?" Reina asked.

Manny thought she was sounding a little too casual. "It's good, I got some stuff," he said.

"Oh, so what did you get?"

Manny was thinking she was sounding a little too perky, but, if he challenged her on it—and she came back at him—well, it would be just another needless scrap that he could avoid— something that would prevent him from dropping a dime on Eugene Close, the dope smuggler.

"I've got some evidence on this hermit," Manny said.

"What kind of evidence you got, big fella?"

130

Manny didn't like the way that sounded, either. Too happy, too offhand. "He's stashing bales of dope in the storage building behind his house. One of the local punks is bringing it to him on a quad. You know me but I know you too, so what is it?"

"I knew something bad was going to happen so I called you. Don't turn him in. It's not just about it's creepy to turn somebody in for marijuana, Manny. It's something else, so please stay out of it, just this once. We'll get hurt if we're in it—you and me, our love, our relationship. Please just let it go, don't call it in. I'll help you find out why he acted the way he did when you showed him pictures of Lois and Evelyn—"

"*¡Tranquilo!* Okay?"

"I'm sorry to be this way, but this is a strong message I'm getting here, Manny."

"I'll do what you say. No worries. And I'll be over there in a little while. Just take it easy. I'll be there shortly."

Manny thought about how he could question this freaking nutcase hermit without violating his promise to Reina. She was psychic, he knew that for sure, and he would honor her, but he hated working under the influence of information that came from the twilight zone, spookville, beyond the veil…. No way could he write stuff like that in reports or testify to it in court—"Uh, no, Your Honor, I didn't turn this asshole in, thereby violating the conditions under which I was given my private investigator's license, because my girlfriend is precognitive and she said it would damage our relationship."

He'd thought of a deal he might work with Reina by the time he'd left his house. The most useful images of the hermit, the punk, the quad, and the dope were now in a flash drive, hanging around his neck by a cord.

*　　*　*　　*

Twenty minutes later, Manny was at Reina's house saying, "So you don't even want me to go out there, show this jerk these pictures of himself stashing dope, and tell him I'll let it go if he tells me what he knows about Lois and Evelyn—is that right?"

"No."

"Then what do I do, Reina?"

"Wait. I know it'll come clear." She stepped in close. "I *know*, Manny."

***

It came clear the next afternoon when Officer Tellez called Manny from Ajo. Manny was on his way to yet another witness interview. He pulled his truck over and listened.

"You asked us about a guy living out toward Charley Bell Pass—a guy who lived all by himself, remote little ranch. You remember?"

Manny remembered.

"Thought you'd like to know. I was part of a raid on his place. We combined with a couple of other agencies to do it. The Border Patrol learned he'd been working with smugglers when they busted one of the local kids out on the Cabeza Prieta Wildlife Refuge. The old guy figured out we were closing in on him and he ran. He came roaring out his back door on a dirt bike. We pursued. He ran that bike right onto the Goldwater Range during a night fire exercise. We broke off pursuit and called the Air Force but it was too late.

"One of the BP guys saw it from a long way off," Tellez continued. "Said it was just this bike with the guy on it, just a tiny silhouette out there, and then the A-10 came down on a target right where the bike was. Remember I told you those rounds go out at 3,900 per minute and it looks like somebody's laying down a bed of hot coals when they hit? BP guy said the light just ate the bike. He thought he saw a wheel fly off. Wheels on fire, rollin' down the road, Manny, and that was all she wrote. We were out there all night, looking for pieces. Paperwork was a nightmare. Did you ever get any intel on the guy?"

"Not much," Manny said. "I got his name. I found out he had no criminal record. He looked nervous when I showed him photographs of Lois Donahue and Evelyn Antone. Did you hear anything about a connection with those women?"

Officer Tellez replied in the negative. Manny was glad he hadn't dropped the fateful dime on Eugene Close. If he had done that, Manny reflected, and it had caused the old man's death, it might have been the end of his relationship with Reina. Manny had killed people. He knew what that could do to relationships. Kill, or get somebody killed, and others looked at you different. From there, it could be just a hop, skip, and a jump to divorces and suicides. Now, he'd have to take his medicine—in the form of telling Reina about it. Some days, he felt like having 'You were right again, Reina' tattooed on his forehead, just to save time.

***

Reina took it pretty easy on him that night, over Chinese takeout and in front of the television, when he told her about Close.

"Another drug war casualty. Drug offenders *and* law enforcement people die in this war. It's meaningless and it's shameful," Reina said, stabbing her chopsticks into pile of gyoza. She paused and looked up. "Did Tellez really say, 'Wheels on fire, rollin' down the road?'"

"Yeah," Manny said, staring at an overcooked piece of cheap beef he'd stuck on his fork.

"That *was* funny," Reina admitted. "But you can't bring somebody back from the dead, Manny." She pointed her chopsticks at him.

"Bring him back?" Manny said. "They couldn't even find him."

***

Manny was sitting in his corner of Goldman's office, reviewing witness statements, when his cell phone vibrated. It didn't even register in Manny's mind, at first, that George's van had left town, presumably with George in it. Manny had gotten dozens of text messages from the GPS he'd put in George's van. He was ready to tell himself to hang it up, that George's appearance on a lot of video tape at the Ban 'eldag Café was a fluke.

"George is leaving town," Manny said to Reina, who was seated at her desk, doing maintenance on reference files. "I talked to Coyote Bob yesterday. There's nothing new with the TO police on the Ban 'eldag murders. George is still a suspect in my book." He started for the door.

"Stay in touch," Reina said. She looked up. "And stay out of trouble."

"Love you, baby," Manny said, heading out the door.

"Not as much as you love chasing cases," Reina called after him.

***

Interstate Ten, between Tucson and Phoenix, was a soul stealing two hour run. The highway was nearly straight, flat, heavily traveled, and well maintained. A lot of the country on either side of the highway was featureless, ugly. Tucson and Phoenix averaged 350 days of sunshine per year. Visibility was usually unlimited, unless there was a dust storm in the cotton farming country north of Picacho Peak. Any extensive breaks in the desert crust created a zero visibility dust storm waiting to happen. Farming provided those breaks. Manny could see basin and range for miles in all directions, laid out under the kind of bright blue skies produced by a total absence of any moisture in the air. He didn't bother maintaining a visual on George's van. The GPS would take care of it. Manny closed in just before the van stopped moving at a location in north Phoenix.

Environmentalists got mad just looking out of airplane windows when they flew over Phoenix. Millions of people, spread out over a square mile area bigger than Los Angeles, in a desert with an average annual rainfall of eight inches. Environmentalists had a word for that: "Nonsustainable." But Phoenix, one of the ten largest cities in the nation, didn't care. More people were moving there. People who lived in Phoenix were working too hard at surviving to worry about theories of sustainability, too ignorant know about it, or too rich to care.

Manny couldn't get into the compound where George parked. The entryway was open, but the place was fenced, and there was razor wire on top of the fences. The low slung white building, made of tin and insulation, looked like a warehouse because of the absence of any real windows and the presence of a big door and a loading dock for trucks. It wasn't a huge building. A dozen pov's—privately owned vehicles in law enforcement jargon—sat in a nicely paved parking space around the perimeter. There were no signs, no indication of what the place was about.

Manny parked across the street and checked out the level of vehicle traffic in the area. There was no foot traffic. George was already inside. Manny was missing out on the conversation. He took a chance in a daylight situation and cranked up a parabolic listening device, a black dish twenty inches wide which could pick up and isolate sounds as far away as 300 yards.

Manny took a brief, unintentional audio tour of the building's interior before he was able to key in on George's voice. Manny listened while scanning the street. When a Phoenix Police Department SUV drove by he had to shove the dish down on the floor and pretend to be looking at a street atlas while hoping the earphones he was wearing just made him look like a million other tuned out citizens.

Between the conversation, oblique as it was—something about "no more deliveries" and "I'm working on logistics," and the sounds of machinery and the talk from the men, apparently machinists, in the main part of the building, Manny understood that George was talking to a firearms manufacturer.

Manny got a break when one of the machinists mentioned a specific metal part that almost certainly belonged to an AR—the Armalite Rifle, famous, common, with several variants and any number of manufacturers, the rifle had been sent all over the world, mostly by the United States. The military variants included the M16 and the M4.

Over the years, the United States had given and sold

thousands of M16's to the governments of Mexico—and Guatemala, on the southern border of Mexico, as well as other Latin American countries—countries with large standing armies that were not used for national defense, but, instead, for the subjugation of citizens.   Anybody who cared to look could see that many of these government-owned weapons had found their way into the hands of the drug cartels—but the cartels were always in the market for new weapons. They had the power to shop all over the world, but the safest and most convenient source was the United States.

***

Manny tried to multitask—covertly hold up his twenty-inch dish, catch garbled conversation, and look out for anybody who might spot him at the same time, but the SUV's ripping past him and charging into the building's parking lot, red and blue lights blazing, caught him by surprise.

Black clad gunmen jumped out of the trucks, the letters BATFE prominently displayed on the backs of their bullet proof vests.

He sat still and watched the bust go down, making sure he saw George hustled out in handcuffs, along with a half-dozen other men. When it was clear the federal officers had the area and the suspects secured—meaning they were relaxing their trigger fingers a little—Manny got out of there, pulled into a conveniently located Taco Bell, and called Reina with the news. When they'd gotten at least half of a plan together, Manny hung up, went into the Taco Bell, ordered a plate of chow from the probable undocumented worker behind the counter, wolfed it down, and then headed back for Tucson.

***

"And why would I want to take this man on as a client?" Goldman said, when Reina had finished talking with Manny and had called

George's girlfriend—and had then barged into Jeff's office, and had asked Jeff, seeing as he was a member of the Criminal Justice Act Panel, a statewide list of attorneys who represent clients on federal charges, to represent her meditation buddy, George Amundsen, on federal weapons violations charges, perhaps to include international arms trafficking violations—and who knew what else.

"It's the only way to find out what happened at the Ban 'eldag," Reina said. "We'll never solve those murder cases if George gets another attorney. And can't Manny talk to George on the side? You won't have to know about it. You can do that."

"Yes," Jeff said. "But what if George is a triple murderer? Two of the victims being women," Jeff continued, "and one of the victims having been mutilated and burned—a heinous crime, which, if George were convicted of it, would put him up on a federal death row for killing three Native Americans on federal land, to wit, the Tohono O'odham Nation? And what if someone discovers the fact that evidence in a triple murder case is being withheld, in the form of those CCTV tapes from the Ban 'eldag? If it's in the best interest of the client, we attorneys are willing to represent them on additional charges, but we are tiptoeing around a case here where evidence has already been withheld— by *us*, meaning those CCTV tapes."

"It won't come to that, Jeff. It can't. George is one of the good guys. At least he's a good enough man not to murder a woman and cut off her finger to get a ring. He would never murder anyone. I think I know him that well. I truly do."

"I'll tentatively agree to take his case, Reina, based on what you've told me. I will need to see what they've charged him with before I can completely accept this risky proposition you've presented to me. You've called his companion and she will get word to him to ask for me when he is given the opportunity to seek counsel?"

"Yes, and thank you, Jeff."

"And his companion—her name?" Jeff was scribbling on a legal pad now.

"Dorothy."

"His companion, Dorothy, had not yet heard from George so you called her and said, 'Tell him to ask for Jeff Goldman when he is given the opportunity to seek representation.' Is that correct?"

"Yes." Reina was keeping it simple. The situation, in her estimation, was so grave that not even jokes could, at the moment, be part of it.

"And you had not yet consulted with me on this when you told this Dorothy person to do that, right?" Goldman gave Reina a severe look from behind his legal pad.

"Well..." Reina said.

"Never mind," Goldman said, waving his pen above his legal pad. "Federal law enforcement may have already taken George for a pre-trial appearance. They have forty-eight hours to do it. They often do it same-day when they make an arrest. We'll know where we can find him after that—at the federal pre-trial detention facility in Florence, Arizona. If this works and I am appointed as counsel, I will review the charges and I will drive to Florence and do an initial meeting with the client. Subsequently, I will do what is necessary to have my investigator, Manuel Aguilar, cleared and sent to Florence. He will further interview the client. And that's all the time we have for today, Reina. I will now leave the office. I have a date with my current love interest, the woman you call 'the prosecutor.'"

"I could kiss you, Jeff," Reina said, "but lips that touch prosecutors will never touch mine."

"But I had you there for a minute, didn't I?" Jeff said. "You were stressed and without jokes." He pointed his pen at her. "You were *jokeless*."

"It's too true, Jeff," Reina said. "Too true."

Chapter Seventeen

"It's better than we thought," Jeff Goldman said, stepping through the front door of the Goldman Law Firm, and letting in bright sunshine and warm air as he did so. May in Arizona was a lot like July in other places. Jeff gestured for his employees to follow him into his office.

"The feds charged our guy George Amundsen with relatively minimal stuff," Jeff said. "George was lucky. He hadn't loaded up any of those machine guns, assault rifles, whatever you want to call them, in his van." Goldman held up a warning finger. "But he may have intended to. I'll let Manny talk to him about that, but I don't have to know George's entire back story to defend him. George was at that firearms manufacturing facility, as far as his defense is concerned, to visit an Army buddy."

"What the hell!" Reina said.

"Yes, it's true. He knew this guy from the Korean War days and the guy was very smart, technically savvy, good head for business—wild about guns, just loved 'em. He manufactures M16's—or whatever you call them."

"AR's," Manny said. "The semiautomatic model of the M16 is the AR15."

"Okay, fine," Goldman said. "But the gun maker, George's old Army buddy, guy by the name of Melvin Amsel—and, not surprisingly, everybody called him Mel—Mel couldn't resist a little late night lab project, consisting of making high quality fully automatic rifles with no markings on them at all. Naturally, he wanted to share his beneficial creations with the world—for a price. He got to talking with George, and George became a buyer, apparently. The feds aren't charging George with that because they don't know it. The feds were after—"

"Mel!" Reina exclaimed.

"And the feds certainly got Mel," Goldman went on, "and they did it because Phoenix PD busted one of Mel's machinists for methamphetamine. Phoenix PD thought the BATFE might want to talk to this machinist. The BATFE flipped the machinist and the guy kept working for Mel and gathering evidence. The feds didn't like Mel's operation much in the first place, apparently, because they had previously heard talk about it on the street."

"But Mel wouldn't inform on George when the arrests were made," Manny said.

"Yes," Goldman said. "That's right. And you can bet the feds spent a lot of time trying to convince George to tell them everything he knew about Mel. Neither man would rat out the other. Manny, you are cleared to interview George. You are acting as my agent and attorney-client privilege applies. Make sure they give it to you—no recordings, no cameras. This is would be a perfect job for Reina because she knows George, but you're the one with the PI license."

***

"George, you had me fooled," Manny said, leaning back in his chair and crossing his arms.

"Well, I had everybody fooled," George said, smiling a gentle smile.

"Reina says hi," Manny said.

George nodded. "Tell her hi for me."

"Jeff is working on your case. The feds don't have much. They're stacking charges on you to pressure you to give them your Army buddy."

George nodded, still smiling. His look said he understood the tactic.

"George, I came to you for advice about Ajo a while ago. You helped me out. Donald Donahue was the husband, the defendant—a Tohono O'odham guy."

George nodded. "Yeah, I remember. Get on with it." He was smiling again.

"Donald got off the charge. The Border Patrol saw him elsewhere that day. He couldn't have killed his wife. But nobody knows who killed her. Later, her sister, Evelyn, was murdered. Then, Albert Azarola." Manny uncrossed his arms and leaned forward. "I know you were good friends with Albert Azarola, George. I'm not going to tell you how I know that but I can prove it in court if I have to."

"Jeff told me you might have some questions that didn't have to do with my case," George said.

"My questions may or may not have anything to do with your case," Manny said. "It depends on your answers. Your relationship with Albert Azarola is not known by the FBI and the Tohono O'odham investigators. If you can tell me anything about Albert—"

"You can quit tiptoeing around," George said. "You don't know Dorothy. She's my girlfriend. Reina told Dorothy what you wanted and Dorothy kind of filled me in as much as she could with all the conversation monitoring they've got going here. You think maybe I killed somebody or I know who did."

"That's right," Manny said. "Reina does not believe you would hurt anybody—"

George raised his hand to shut Manny up. "Albert killed Lois. They were having an affair. When Lois heard Donald was coming out of the state pen she broke it off. Albert wasn't having it. He went *nuts*, seeing her every day at the café. He used to talk to me about it. He was crazy. I knew about Lois's murder—everybody did, it was in the newspapers. Then Evelyn, Lois's sister. I heard about that. I thought maybe Albert did that one, too. I dropped by the gallery one night and we were talking in back. He was tossing a wedding ring up in his hand and catching it. He was telling me he killed Lois. He picked up a framing hammer and came at me. I just shot him right there. I made it look like a robbery."

"Can you prove that?"

"Why would I want to?" George asked. "*You* can't prove it and neither could the cops."

Manny's only reaction was another question. "Can you prove you didn't kill Lois Donahue?"

"I was at the Coyote Howls that whole day. People saw me."

"How about Evelyn Antone?"

"Now you're getting kind of silly," George said.

"I don't have any choice, George. You just told me you killed Albert Azarola—only you say it was self-defense—and maybe it was—but if you killed one person, maybe you killed two or three. You're a smart guy. You know I have to ask these questions." Manny recited the date of Evelyn Antone's death. "Where were you the day Evelyn Antone was killed?"

"Coyote Howls, I think," George said. "People would have seen me. You can ask out at the Howls."

"How did you get to know Albert so well?"

"Ah, you're a funny kid," George said. "I used to interrogate people, too, back in my Army days. I got to know Albert because I like Native art." George smiled.

Manny could see George was enjoying himself. A couple of cogs clicked in Manny's brain and he realized George was typical of a certain type of bright criminal—someone who couldn't stop himself from fooling other people—a childish trait.

Manny had discussed this idea with Reina. Reina had noticed people like that, too. She believed it was genetic, that they'd find a cure one day, and so on. At least, Manny thought, this was one case where Reina didn't start citing the influence of supernatural forces. Manny himself simply believed in identifying such people and hunting them down like dogs when they inevitably committed a criminal act.

"We were talking one day and the topic turned to guns," George said. "Albert had the route through the reservation to Mexico and a good cover for traveling around—he was an art dealer. He might be anywhere on the rez at almost any time, buying and transporting art. I had the connection up in Phoenix. We both made good money for a while. That's when I was living out at the Coyote Howls. Lois Donahue used to do courier runs for us. When Albert collected the money, she'd run it out to me in Why—she'd bring her kid with her—a good cover. I used to give him toys."

"Lois never went to Ajo?"

"Not that I know of," George said. "That wouldn't have been a good idea. Too many cops up there."

"Who killed Evelyn Antone?"

"I haven't the slightest idea," George said. He was still smiling when the corrections officer appeared and escorted him away.

Manny went out through a few heavy doors and a fence with silvery barb wire on top.

He drove the two-lane from Florence to Tucson. Once there, he laid out George's story for Jeff and Reina. The three of them kicked it around. When they were done kicking they left the office, carrying the weight of secrets.

***

The next morning Manny prepared to leave Reina's house for yet another three-hour trip to Ajo. He'd called the management at the Coyote Howls. They were welcoming, as usual. They believed they could verify George Amundsen's alibi for Lois and Evelyn's murders. They would ask other residents of the Howls and be ready to direct Manny to those persons when he arrived. When he hit the off button on his cell phone his mind caught on the little fixed blade knife Beck wore, the knife with the word 'Walker' written inside the belt loop. He realized he no longer expected to find an answer for that question.

He would never have told Reina he was going to try to see Walker again if he thought he could get away with keeping secrets from her. "I'm going to see Walker," he muttered, his head stuck into the refrigerator on the pretext of looking for a stack of flour tortillas.

"Why?" Reina said, cat's eyes behind a coffee cup.

"Walker gave us some information that helped us. That's one thing."

"And?"

"I showed people in Ajo pictures of Evelyn Antone and Lois Donahue. Law enforcement out there recognized Evelyn—just

143

about everybody recognized Evelyn—except for Walker. And Walker knows everybody in town. Beck, the drug counselor, sent me to him. Walker's the go-to guy for scuttlebutt—he's a reporter. A guy named Dacey—works for the Copper News— recognized Evelyn Antone when I showed him her picture. She'd been in there. I want to know if Dacey sent her to Walker."

Reina shook her head and put her coffee cup down. "Why would Walker know anything about Evelyn Antone being murdered on a rez—"

"Now you're saying it."

"Saying what?"

"*Rez.*"

"...being murdered on a *rez*," Reina continued, "a hundred miles from Ajo? You're telling me you're going to challenge this old spook because he might be lying about seeing Evelyn Antone? And how could you prove it if he did? By the way, I hope you're not going in there wearing a wire." She pushed the black coffee cup away from her and lifted her eyes, giving him a cold look. "Or a gun."

Manny was standing in the kitchen now, pouring himself a second cup of coffee. "I may not be able to prove anything. I talked to Dacey at the Copper News. Walker's been in their office this morning and he's supposed to be reporting on some kind of event in town. I'm sure he'll be around—and I'm not wearing a wire or a gun."

"Yeah, well," Reina said, "so you're telling me you just want to ask kindly old Mr. Walker if he's sure he's never seen Evelyn Antone. You better meet him in a public place."

Chapter Eighteen

Chuck Dacey, like the rest of the Copper News staff, was busy getting the paper out when Manny stepped into the newspaper's book and stationary store on Pajaro Street. Manny reintroduced himself and, once again, took out a photo of Evelyn Antone.

"You said she'd been in your offices, asking about something. Do you remember what you told her?"

Dacey thought for a minute. "I told her to go see Bill Walker," he said.

***

Manny drove up the hill past the Curley School, laboriously turned his old truck around in the street, and parked on the curb, facing downhill. He caught movement in his rearview mirror and watched while another truck with two men in it pulled to the curb and stopped thirty feet behind him. On the way up the hill he'd caught a glimpse of a sullen kid on a cell phone, lounging alone on the steps of a church.

"Come in," Walker called when Manny knocked on the painted wooden door of Walker's house, a door painted a color common in the desert, a flat kind of grayish red, like clay.

There was no light to speak of inside the house. The light there was came from a small window on the north side of the room and from another small window on the east wall. The sun was well past the east window, taking its time moving west, baking the white buildings of Ajo in the still afternoon.

William Walker sat in his chair by the east window, half of him in the deeper shadow the window light failed to reach. Across the room, in a corner, another man sat completely in shadow. Manny could see that the man's pale eyes were fixed on him. Walker gestured at a chair by the door and Manny sat down there, between the stranger and Walker.

"I just talked to Chuck Dacey over at the Copper News. I asked him about Evelyn Antone again. He remembered he'd sent her to you. You're everywhere in this town, you know everybody, and you're about the only person in Ajo who said he didn't recognize Evelyn Antone when I showed you her picture."

"Well," Walker said, "you know we had to do her in."

Manny felt a zip of electricity start somewhere around his ass, blast up the center of his body, pound through his forebrain, and stop just above his eyes. It had happened before when he'd done things like step on a rattlesnake or have a gun pulled on him.

"She was quite the little detective, Manny—oh, he's deaf," Walker said, waving a hand at the pale-eyed man in the corner. Walker tipped his head toward the man again to emphasize his point. "Would you believe it? He reads lips real well in Spanish and English, and he's an absolute psychopath—best I've ever seen." Walker shook his head in admiration. "Now Manny, let's just leave well enough alone. Let's just say certain goods need to go to the right people, and not to the competition just because some fool decided to go into business—" Walker paused to chuckle "—for himself. No point in you going on about it because it's gonna' go on. Sleeping dogs, son. Let it lie."

"So you got that piece of crap in the corner to kill Evelyn Antone?" Manny said, shifting just enough in the chair so the gunman couldn't read his lips. "Why?"

"Heck, I just told you, Manny," Walker said. "Now, before you go any further, peek out the window for me, will you?"

"I saw your guys in the truck," Manny said. "I'm not peeking out any windows."

"Well, there's a Border Patrol truck out there now, Manny," Walker said. "And it's ready to take you out to the Devil's Highway—about eighty miles west of here, if you go the back way—which my man will do, meaning my Border Patrol officer." Walker's face lit up in a smile. "I got to have one of them working for *me*. The cartels got three or four in the Yuma sector alone.

"What say I have my man drive you out to a spot in the

Tinajas Altas Mountains—the high tanks, it means in Spanish. The Devil's Highway runs right by it. People been dying on that road for a *long* time. Those tanks, those big holes in the decayed granite out there hold the only year-round water for seventy miles. There's graves around the tanks. Rings of stones. Little crosses made out of pebbles. You'd fit right in—dead, that is." Walker shifted in his chair, pointing his sharp old knees at Manny and Manny could see the Browning, then—the dark pistol held along Walker's thigh. "The real deal, though," Walker said, "is we both know I won't need my man to haul your ass away because you're gonna walk out of here on your own—for the simple reason that Evelyn Antone is dead, you'll never in million years prove I had her killed, and, best of all, no cop would believe it if you told 'em. You can't prove anything. And, Manny, I'm protected. I'm part of the United States government's furniture out here. I'm under the cloak. Trying to rat me out would be un-American."

Manny leaned forward in his chair, rested his elbows on his thighs, and looked up at Walker. "Let's suppose you're not as crazy as I think you are. You got that idiot in the corner with a gun. You've got those goons outside—and that little *halcon* down the street. I know that much. So, why'd you kill Evelyn Antone if you're the grand poobah of black ops in Ajo?"

"You're puttin' up a good front, Manny, I'll give you that," Walker said. "My real name is DeForest Sayles and I do contract work for the United States of America—but you can call me Walker. Everybody else does. William Walker, class of 1964, University of Virginia Cavaliers, *a su servicio*. You're the anomaly here—one of them *detective heroes*.

"We killed Evelyn because she had that Indian thing going for her and she got close enough to one of my guys here in town that he spilled the beans to her about what we do here. Evelyn was quite the little detective. She knew her sister Lois was doing something illegal. Thing was, Evelyn thought Lois was doing whatever it was in Ajo, not in Why. So Evelyn showed up here and made our lives miserable—until we killed her. Now, we didn't kill

Lois Donahue. You know that, but we could not have her little sister Evelyn puttin' a light on us. We killed the guy who told Evelyn about us and then we killed Evelyn. Why? Because she could get them Indians riled up. Indians don't like to cooperate. We run our guns through Lukeville, mostly. Some of our stuff we run across the reservation. We need access to the reservation, but we don't need a bunch of Indians knowin' who we are. Evelyn had one of them Shadow Wolves for a boyfriend—and I'll bet you thought a little old gal with horn rimmed glasses didn't have a life, didn't you? Evelyn would likely have told them Shadow Wolves about my operation. We got the Border Patrol and the Pima County Sheriffs buffaloed. If they arrest one of our guys they soon find out he's DEA and on a secret mission, and a confidential informant, and all of that shit and they let him go. They get the word from higher up. Done deal. The Indian cops—federal Indian cops like the Shadow Wolves? Maybe not a done deal after all— and them regular Indians? They're even more of a pain in the ass. They got do gooders and social activists amongst 'em. Bleedin'-hearted pansies."

"So you killed her?"

"Yup. Had Melchor over there do it," Walker said, pointing at the man in the corner. "And I should thank you for helping me, Manny. If it hadn't been for you, foolin' around, I wouldn't have had such a good shot at taking down old George and his arms dealer buddy. Those old geeks were my competitors. I don't need that. I do guns for drugs, man. It's country simple. The intelligence community in this country cannot present a budget to congress for everything we do. We need the money. I came up in the old flyin' days, in Air America, in 'nam. We flew the heroin to finance ourselves. These days, we got Afghanistan—and the heroin's been flowin' ever since we been there—just ask a Kazakh, one of them folks that lives a country or two north of Afghanistan. They all know the drugs been rolling through their little nation on the way to market. This post-911 war fever boom? This here 'ultra-nationalism'? It's been good to us. Kind of a present to me in my golden years after all that stuff about somethin' bein' wrong with

Vietnam." Walker grinned and brushed the back of his hand across his nose. He leaned forward, toward Manny, and his look became serious and intent. "Mexico is *our* business, Manny. Latin America is *our* hemisphere. This country needs one particular cartel we got out here in western Arizona. We need our cartel to beat them other cartels out of the drug routes. Old Mel and George didn't know it but they was supplying our competition. How in the *hell* do you think these Mexican cartel bosses stay *alive* out here, anyway? Our black ops guys could of took 'em out years ago. We need that income stream from Mexican drugs. The cartels need guns. You helped us put a rival gun runner out of business. Now things are back to normal. Thank you. If you report all of this shit you'll be laughed off the face of the earth." Walker waved a hand at the door. "Now you go on and have yourself a nice day." Walker sat back in his chair, his unmarked Browning in his hand, barrel resting lengthwise on his thigh, and the blue-eyed psychopath in the corner sat in the same way as Walker and never blinked.

"Eugene Close," Manny said, "that guy who lived out by Charley Bell Pass. He worked for you, didn't he?"

"He did and didn't know it," Walker said. He smiled. "Pawn in the game, Mr. Detective Hero. Don't let it happen to you." Walker tipped his head toward the door.

Manny knew that if he'd been eighteen years old, he'd have tried to kill them both. He got up and opened the painted wooden door of Walker's house and went across the street to his truck and drove off down the hill. The bright white buildings of Ajo had a haunted look, as though the sunshine itself had a mysterious something in its light.

Lois Donahue was dead. Her killer was dead. Her little sister's killers were beyond justice. William Walker was more than a shadow. He was darkness itself. Manny Aguilar had solved three murders and uncovered a government conspiracy—and he couldn't prove any of it. He considered his options. He might have committed suicide and killed Walker right there in Walker's house—result being another spook would float in and take

Walker's place and Manny himself would join the dead out west of town. Reina would know, but that would be all—unless she, in one of her visions, could see under the dirt in the Lechuguilla Desert, out on the Devil's Highway.

Manny thought about telling the Tohono O'odham—but he was a stranger, a Latino, a non-Indian, a disgraced ex-cop, who would be telling Native Americans about a government conspiracy. He would be lucky if laughter was the only response he got.

Now he knew how far the tunnels under the shining face of his country drilled down in the dark. There was no bottom. He'd never get the stink off. He was part of it now. But Donald Donahue didn't have to be. For all the time Donny had spent in prison, and for the bullets Manny had fired into his ribs, Donny could be left alone to do the simple, important things. He could raise his son, ride his horse in his own country, and remember his wife.

The sheriff's officers were sitting in their white trucks at the little triangle at the bottom of town. Manny lifted a hand to them as he passed. The honorable and the strong would hunt what the laws commanded them to hunt until the laws were changed. The weak and the bad would use the badge to steal dope and money and take bribes. The weather was hot. Summer in the desert— what these lawmen called 'the dead body season.'

Manny drove down State Route 85, past the pile of the earth's guts, heaved up from the copper mine. He rolled on across the downward sloping desert and turned east at Why.

***

Sylvia Mendez was sweeping the stockroom in the rear of the art gallery when her broom chased Lois Donahue's wedding ring out from under a cabinet. The new art gallery manager, yet another dick in Sylvia's opinion, at least trusted her to work in the gallery section of the Ban 'eldag Café and Art Gallery.

Sylvia picked up the ring and cruised into the bathroom. She put the ring on the third finger of her right hand, next to her favorite ring, a Tyrannosaurus Rex head snarling in sterling silver, and checked it out in the mirror, holding her hand in front of the crossed pistols tattooed on her chest.

"Meh," Sylvia said. She carried the ring out to the stockroom and gently toed it back underneath the cabinet. She had a pretty good idea where it had come from.